Trusting

(South Coast Bro   . #3)

Kacey Hamford

LOVE

K. Hamford x

Text copyright © 2016

Kacey Hamford

Table Of Contents

Acknowledgements

I really enjoyed writing this book and there are a few people who made it possible.

Firstly my better half, for allowing me the peace and quiet to write and not complaining when I wake up in the middle of the night to jot down ideas as the book characters just won't let me sleep.

Stef, for always telling me she needs to read more after I've sent her a few chapters and for helping me write my fabulous synopsis.

Lucii, my PA and friend, for always encouraging me.

Bonnie, Kathleen, Emma, Titian and Michelle for supporting me in my writing and for giving me honest opinions on the book when Beta reading.

For the girls in my street team, Kacey's Kick Ass Crew for helping get my name out there and always supporting me.

Finally, thank you to you, the reader for buying this book. I hope you enjoy the third instalment of the South Coast Brothers.

Prologue

Cammie

I was always a wild child, even from a young age. I remember never having rules, a set bed time, a curfew. I was always allowed to do as I pleased. I felt, as an only child, my parents never took on the role seriously; I was never disciplined and could quite easily bunk off school whenever I wanted to. I put that down to the fact that my mum and dad were only young when they had me. My dad was nineteen and my mum only eighteen, they were crazy in love and when both of their families told them to get rid of me, they argued that they wanted me. Both of their families disowned them and that's how I grew up in Devon.

I remember being as young as ten and my parents leaving me home alone while they went partying, I learnt to feed and look after myself quickly. Naturally, I followed in their footsteps. I hung out with the wrong crowd, never done any school work, started drinking and smoking by the time I was fourteen.

"Mum, dad? I have something to tell you." I looked at them as they sat on the sofa together, holding hands, watching TV. My sixteen year old self may as well have been invisible for all they cared.

"Well? Spit it out?" Mum snapped.

"Um, well... I'm pregnant."

"What!" My dad bellowed as he climbed to his feet and looked at me. This was the most attention he had showed me in the last few months.

"Who done this to you? Was it rape? Were you forced? Was it that Jeremy guy?" Mum rattled off question after question, not giving me a chance to speak as she looked in my direction but not directly at me.

"No, Mum, I…"

"I'm calling the police. If it was that Jeremy, he's nearly twice your age and he'll go down for rape," my dad said as he paced the floor. I was surprised by their reaction, I didn't actually think they would care. I had got used to them not caring about me in the last six years.

"It wasn't Jeremy and there was no forcing. I want this baby." I looked at them, hoping to reason with them. If anyone should understand it would be them, they knew what it was like not to have the support of your family.

"We'll talk about this tomorrow, honey, our programme is starting," mum said. I turned away from them and walked out of the front door, straight into the arms of Jack.

Jack had been my boyfriend for about six months. We met one evening when I was sitting in the empty playground that was at the end of our street. I was swinging gently on the swings, drinking cider. He was older than me by three years, his square jaw, dark hair and brown eyes drew me in. He once told me that I was beautiful, that my long, blonde hair was like sunshine and my bright blue eyes were like the sea. He looked after me and I craved that attention after feeling non-existent in my home.

"They didn't take it well?" he asked as he steered me towards his black, rusted old car.

"No. Dad thinks I was raped and mum was too concerned with missing her TV programme." I was about to climb in the car when he stopped me by the tight grip he had on my arm.

"What? I hope you told them I didn't rape you, that you wanted it as much as I did."

"Of course I told them that it wasn't rape. I want this baby. We'll be fine." I stretched up on my tiptoes and gave him a kiss. "We will be fine, right?"

"Yeah," he replied on a sigh. "You coming to mine?" I nodded quickly, biting my lip. I loved all the attention he showed me and the ways he made my body burn up from the inside.

***

I was just over eight months pregnant and living with Jack and his two roommates in a small three bedroom flat. None of them worked, all they did all day was sit around watching TV, drinking and smoking. I had a job at a restaurant in town for a little while, but as I was so big now I was finding it difficult to manoeuvre easily around the tables so I had to quit. My ankles were constantly swollen and standing up for long periods of time was becoming painful.

We found out that we were having a boy and I was extremely excited. Jack? Not so much. I had tried to get him to help me pick a name for him but he wasn't interested so I decided on the name Noah.

I struggled up the three flights of stairs with bags of shopping so we had some food in the flat. We were on limited funds so I had to buy the basic food we needed to survive. Once I reached the top step, I had to stop for a breather. I could hear loud music and shouting coming from the down the hall and I hoped whoever was having a party that it wouldn't be a late one, I was tired and needed some sleep. As I got closer to our flat, I saw that the front door was open and it was filled with loud music and people drinking and smoking. I pushed my way in and headed to the kitchen where I saw Jack all over another woman. She was older than me with bleached blonde hair with hardly any clothing on. I dropped the bags to the floor, causing the milk to split open and pour all over the stained flooring.

"Shit!" I heard Jack say before he pushed the woman away

and took a step closer to me. "I didn't think you would be home yet," he slurred. How much had he had to drink? It was only seven in the evening.

"Clearly. How long has this been going on?" I waved my hand between him and the bleached blonde tart standing near us.

"I'm only having a bit of fun," he said, laughing. "Now that you can't move around as easily."

"I'm carrying your son." I poked him hard in the chest.

"Yeah and I didn't ask for that!" he shouted. I cowered back from him, I couldn't believe what I was hearing. He had been distant with me lately, I was starting to feel ignored and invisible again but I knew it would all be ok once our son arrived. Jack would see how special he was and realise that we all needed each other. We would be a proper family. His words hurt me, I wanted to cry but I wouldn't give him the satisfaction of seeing them. I turned around and headed for the front door, I would come back once the party was over and hopefully Jack would be ready to apologise.

I made it down two flights of stairs but I needed a moment to catch my breath. I leant against the cold stone wall, closed my eyes and concentrated on breathing. Noah was kicking me and I placed my hand on my tummy to feel it more, there was nothing stronger than a bond between a mum and her baby.

"What the hell are you doing?" My eyes snapped open as I heard Jack's fierce voice.

"Trying to breathe." I stood up straight and started making my way down the last set of steps when he grabbed hold of the top of my arm, halting me.

"Where the hell do you think you're going?" he snapped.

"Away from here, from this party, go and have your fun. I'll be back later." I tried to pull my arm free and his grip tightened.

"You're not leaving me," he growled.

"I'll be back later." I pulled my arm and he let me go, I stumbled, lost my footing and fell down the rest of the stairs. I pulled my arms around my tummy trying to protect my son. I felt the bump of each step, it felt like I was moving in slow motion until I felt the solid ground under me and a sharp pain shoot up through my back. I cried out and laid still, waiting for Jack to come and help me. I didn't know how long I waited but he never came.

Chapter 1

Cammie

My life hasn't always been easy. I experienced a pain no one should ever have to go through. A part of me would always be broken, a piece of my heart shattered the day I had to give birth to my stillborn son.

"Cammie, bedroom! Now!" Mason, the VP of the Cornish Crusaders called out to me as he stormed into the clubhouse. His dark hair was messy from wearing his helmet, the sun shone off his lip ring and his hands were fisted tightly together. We had been together for several weeks and I was seriously falling in love with him but I had never planned to. I had sworn off love for so long I didn't even think I was capable of loving someone, but he tried to show me every day that I was worthy of his love. I loved his no nonsense attitude and after being a club whore for over two years at the Devon Destroyers MC, I knew the rules I had to follow. Do as you're told, no answering back and no asking questions about club business.

I never planned to be a club whore; who wakes up one day and thinks, I know what I'll do for the rest of my life, I'll spread my legs to earn money. Nope, not me. I didn't really have any other choice.

After giving birth to Noah, who was perfect by the way; a head full of light hair, small button nose and pouty lips, I spiralled even more out of control, the hospital called my mum and dad as I was only sixteen. They came and got me, took me to arrange the funeral for Noah and took me back home to live with them. It was almost like they changed who they were overnight. When I left to live with Jack, my parents were glad for me to be gone. They had always ignored me and gone about their lives as if I didn't exist, but they picked me up when I was broken. They were there for me when I needed them the most, but no amount of attention they gave me made up for how they had treated me for the last six years. Nothing helped to fill the gaping hole in my heart that bled for my son. I felt trapped, like I couldn't breathe, I needed to get away from them, from the place that my son was conceived.

As I walked quickly towards Mason, I looked into his eyes. I wasn't sure what I was seeing, was it love? Lust? Anger? I just couldn't tell. When I was close enough to him, he grabbed my hand and began pulling me behind him towards his bedroom.

"VP!" We stopped walking as Solar rushed towards us. He was wearing his usual scruffy jeans, black boots, a tight fitted t-shirt that sat underneath his leather cut. His hair was styled, his short beard was messy and his blue eyes looked worried.

"Solar." Mason nodded his head in greeting.

"Prez called…" He stopped talking and looked at me over Mason's shoulder. All the guys knew that they weren't supposed to talk about club business in front of us. I didn't know if that was a rule in all clubs but we were told it was for our own protection.

I never knew any club business but that didn't stop the Satan MC trying to torture it out of me. After a couple of hours with them, I learnt it was best not to cry and beg them to stop, it was what they liked to hear. After being with them for a day, I learnt to switch off and find a happy place to escape to. That place was with my son, Noah. We were in a park and I was pushing him on the swings, his laughter rang out each time I pushed him higher and higher. The sun would be shining and his blond hair would glisten, the slight breeze causing his fringe to move. Oh, what I would give for that memory to come alive.

"You go ahead, babe. I'll be there in a second." Mason let go of my hand and kissed me briefly on the lips. I turned around and walked away from them slowly, they didn't begin talking until I was almost around the corner. I pushed the door open and walked into the room I now shared with him. The bed was messy, clothes covered the floor on the side he slept and the room was dark and dull due to the sun setting. I didn't know why Mason had demanded we go to his room, was he annoyed? Upset? Or did he want us to finally take the next step in our relationship. I had felt a connection with Mason as soon as Heather and I arrived at the Cornish Crusaders MC, but I hadn't been away from the Satan MC for long and after the way they captured, tortured and raped me I was hesitant about spending time with another man, especially a biker. I knew nothing about him.

Mason looked rough and rugged with all his tattoos and piercings but on the inside he was soft and gentle, he showed me that he cared about me and once I came to the realisation that I had feelings for him too I took a huge leap out of my comfort zone and told him. I hadn't told him about my past, about Noah or the Satan MC, all I said was I needed time and that if he needed a physical relationship straight away that I couldn't be with him. It surprised me as hell when he held my hand and asked if he could hold me, I felt safe wrapped up in his arms.

Now, I wasn't sure what he wanted, he wouldn't have been dragging me to his bedroom if it was only to talk. My heart rate increased, my tummy fluttered and I wasn't sure if it was due to excitement or fear.

I decided I wasn't going to let fear rule my life anymore, I was falling in love with Mason and I knew that he would never hurt me. I pulled the zip down on my skirt and wiggled my way out of it, kicking off my flip flops too. I was glad that I decided to wear a matching set of underwear this morning. I pulled my t-shirt off over my head and examined my body in the full length mirror, my body ran cold when I saw the ugly scar on the side of my tummy. I didn't want Mason seeing it, not yet. I turned to my bedside table and pulled out some lingerie, it was a bright blue babydoll. I slipped it on and loved the fact that it had a v neck so still showed off my breasts and the transparent lace covered my ugly scar but still showed enough skin to drive him wild. I pulled off my black underwear and replaced it with the blue g string that matched. I stood by the door trying to find the sexiest way to look, I tried sitting on the edge of the bed, leaning against the wall, perched on the edge of the dressing table but it all looked too staged. I stood up straight when I heard him yelling.

"Just get it done!"

Seconds later the bedroom door flew open, banging against the wall which made me jump and I was standing in front of him, not looking into his eyes.

"Fuck!" he swore and within seconds I felt his hands on my hips. I trembled and again I wasn't sure if it was from excitement or fear. "Cam, you look fucking hot." I finally looked up into his eyes and they were swimming with desire.

Mason

I don't know what I'd done in a past life to receive such a wonderful gift, I felt like all of my Christmases had come at once when I saw Cammie step out of Heather's car. She looked like a goddess, blonde hair blowing in the wind, blue eyes that sparkled when the sun hit them but her eyes also told me that she was lost. I had to fight the urge not to throw her over my shoulder and make her mine. I was used to getting what I wanted, when I wanted it but something about her told me not to rush it and I just knew that she would be worth the wait.

She came to me a few weeks ago and told me how she felt, she let it all out and I admired her for that, she explained she couldn't have a physical relationship yet, I wanted to know more but she closed herself off and I didn't want to run the risk of scaring her away. I moved her into my room a couple of weeks later and all we had done was kiss, cuddle, touch and sleep in the same bed. No sex. It was pure torture feeling her smooth skin and curves against my body every night and I felt bad that every morning when we woke up she had my hard dick poking her in the back.

Now here she was standing in front of me in a skimpy little outfit and my dick was causing my jeans to tighten. I wanted to touch her so I took a step closer and placed my hands on her hips.

"What are you doing, babe?" I whispered softly into her ear before I kissed the soft skin below it.

"Isn't this what you want?"

"Fuck, yeah but only when you're ready." I pulled back, keeping my hands firmly on her hips and looked into her eyes. I'm not sure what I saw, was it excitement or fear?

"Isn't this why you dragged me back here?" Shit, was that what she thought? I tightened my hands on her hips and at the same time her eyes bulged from her head and I remember what Blade had told me when we were out on the job. I released my hold on her and I think I saw her sigh in relief.

"I wanted to talk to you," I began. I looked her body up and down, man was she sexy and distracting. "I need you to put some clothes on, babe. We need to talk." She nodded and grabbed some clothes and headed into the bathroom. That gave me a chance to think about Blade, Solar, grannies, cats, dogs and anything that would calm my raging hard on.

I sat on the small two seater sofa that was under the window and waited for Cammie to come out of the bathroom. When she stepped out she was wearing jeans and a t-shirt, her hair was piled on top of her head in a messy bun and her face was make-up free, just the way I liked it. She stopped in front of me and I held out my hand for her, she took it and I gently pulled her to sit beside me.

"Everything ok?" she asked.

"Why won't you let me touch you?"

"What?" Her eyebrows rose. "I do let you touch me. I just offered myself to you and you didn't want me."

"Fuck." I shook my head. "Of course I want you. You feel every morning what your body does to mine." She opened her mouth to say something. One thing I loved about her was her smart mouth, she liked to argue and it made me hotter for her. I placed my finger on her lips, silencing her and her tongue darted out to taste me. Shit. If she kept doing that this conversation wouldn't be happening.

"Why didn't you tell me about the Satan's?"

"What?" she whispered, her face paling.

"Blade let slip about them taking you, why didn't you tell me?"

"I don't like to talk about it." She looked at her hands in her lap, talking quietly. I pushed her chin up with my fingers so I could see her bright blue eyes, they were slightly darker now, sadness taking them over.

"I need to hear it."

"Why?" she whispered again.

"Because, Cammie, you're mine. I want to protect you. I want to know everything about you."

"I can't," she sobbed and stood up quickly. Was she running away? I grabbed hold of her wrist and she flinched which made me release her straight away.

"Cam." I sighed as I climbed to my feet, she stopped walking and I strolled slowly towards her. I placed my lips on the top of her head and wound my arms around her, she leant into me, her back to my front.

"I'm sorry, Mason. I can't talk about it, I'm not strong enough."

"How about I ask some questions and you can just nod or shake your head for now?"

"Ok."

I turned her around and cupped her face in my hands. "Just tell me to stop and I will." She nodded and I covered her lips with mine.

Chapter 2

Mason

I wound my arm around Cammie's back and led her back to the sofa. Once we were both seated, the questions started.

"Did they take you from the Devon clubhouse?" She nodded.

"Did they hurt you?" She nodded.

"How long were you there?" She didn't answer. "Was you the only woman there?" She shook her head.

"Do you know who took you?" She nodded. "Who was it?" Still no answer.

"Do you know why they took you?" She nodded as tears started running down her face. "Are you going to tell me?" She shook her head. I was trying to stay calm but I wasn't getting the answers I needed.

"Did they hit you?" She nodded.

"Cut you?" She nodded.

"Make you black out?" She nodded. I needed to ask the last question and I think I already knew the answer, but I needed to know.

"Did they rape you?" She nodded. "All of them?" She nodded and a sob rose from her throat. Fuck. I tried to keep it together, to be able to comfort her but the rage was building in my chest, fighting its way out.

"I'm sorry," she whispered as she face planted my chest and her sobs turned into full blown crying. I held onto her and told her everything would be ok now. Blade had told me that they went in and killed the majority of them and torched their clubhouse but we knew some were still around as they were at the warehouse this morning. I would make it my mission to find and kill every single one of them, and the one that took Cammie from her home would feel every ounce of my rage.

"Cammie, baby. I have something for you." She pulled back from me and I wiped her tears away. I kissed her lips quickly before standing up and walking to my wardrobe. I pulled open the door and routed around until I found the leather jacket that had been sitting in here since I patched in after being a prospect for a year at the Cornish Crusaders, which was nearly ten years ago. I never wanted anyone to have this before and no one else would ever wear it.

"I want you to wear this, babe." I passed her the leather cut that would show everyone that she was mine, and anyone that messed with her would be sorry.

"What? Why?" She looked confused.

"I want everyone to know that you're mine, I want you to be my Old Lady. Will you?"

"No, I can't." She stood up and pushed the jacket back towards me.

"Why can't you?"

"I'm sorry, Mason, I love you but I'm not good enough for you."

"You're the only woman that I want and need in my life. You're better than all the other women that I've met. You're kind, gentle, passionate, loving..."

"Broken, used, dirty..." she interrupted me. She wound her arms around her body and shivered. I didn't hesitate, I walked over to her and wrapped my arms around her, throwing the leather jacket onto the bed behind us.

"You're sexy, smart mouthed, independent and those are just some of the reasons why I love you."

She pulled back and looked at me, the colour in her eyes lighter now. Had I managed to draw her out of the darkness that was threatening to take over?

"You love me?" She smiled.

"Of course I love you, I think I've loved you since the moment you stood up to me and screamed at me to leave you alone. No one has ever stood up to me like that before, scared of the consequences I guess."

"I'm not scared of you," she quietly said.

"Good, I don't want you to be scared of me. I want you to be my Old Lady, forever."

"I can't, not yet." I went to talk and she placed her finger over my lips, I stuck out my tongue to taste her, much like she had done to me. "Mason, we haven't even slept together yet."

"I don't care," I mumbled behind her finger.

"We may not be suited in that department."

"Oh, baby, I know we'll be suited, we'll make love, fuck and move the fucking earth." She smiled and blushed slightly. "So, is that a yes?"

"Not yet, I'll think about it. There's still so much more you don't know about me."

"Then tell me."

"I will, I promise. Just not yet."

"Ok, I'll be patient and wait. But you will be mine and only mine. I'm in love with you, Cammie."

"I'm already only yours but taking the jacket is a big step, one I'm not quite ready for. I love you too, Mason."

Hearing those words come from her mouth was like music to my ears, I've only ever said those words to one other person but it never felt like this. We were only sixteen when we thought we were in love. Now this was the real thing.

"I'm going to see if Heather needs any help with the babies." Cammie stood on her tiptoes and kissed me. Before she could pull away, I wrapped my arm around her back, holding her tight against me. Using my other hand to tilt her head so I could deepen the kiss. After a couple of minutes, she placed her hand on my chest and pushed me back. I managed to pull her hair out of the band that was holding it on top of her head so it was now flowing around her shoulders. I liked it better this way, I liked being able to run my fingers through her hair. It was soft and silky to touch.

"Do you want some lunch?"

"Na, I'm good. Thanks, babe. I'll be out in a minute." I cleared my throat as I adjusted myself in my jeans. I couldn't walk out into the clubhouse sporting a hard on, I'd get a club whore pushed at me.

I watched Cammie run a hair brush over her head and apply some lip gloss, her eyes were still watery from crying but to me she still looked beautiful.

"I'll see you out there." She smiled before she left the room.

I grabbed the dirty clothes off the floor and shoved them into the clothes hamper, made the bed and cleaned up the bathroom. I was doing anything and everything I could to get rid of my excitement, though seeing Cammie again would probably just put me back to stage one again. I loved how my body reacted to hers and I couldn't wait to get her naked and underneath me.

I figured nothing was helping when I was thinking like that so I adjusted myself again and headed for the bar. I stopped dead in my tracks when I heard Cammie talking to Heather.

"Why do you look so surprised? I know I'm not good enough for him. I mean, I've got baggage, I'm a club whore."

"No," Heather told her. I picked up my pace.

"I *do not* want to hear you say that again. Ever!" I bellowed behind them, my hands were fisted tightly by my sides as I stared at them. I walked slowly towards them not taking my eyes off my woman, she dipped her head and once I reached her I pushed her chin up so she had to look at me.

"You are *not* a club whore. You're my Old Lady. Got it?"

"I haven't said yes yet," she softly spoke and I growled in response.

"You will." I kissed her quickly before walking away and into the bar.

Chapter 3

Cammie

I hated watching my best friend Heather leave. She was on her way back to Devon with her family. Blade had to get back to his club and Heather wanted their kids settled in their own house. She begged me to go back with her but I knew I was in the place that I needed and wanted to be. The thought of walking away and leaving Mason made my chest ache, I was in love with him and I owed it to myself to see if I could truly be happy here with him.

"Morning," Mason grumbled as he wrapped his arms around me from behind and nuzzled his unshaven face into my neck.

"Morning. Do you want some coffee?" I asked as I poured some coffee into a cup for myself.

"Yes, please, babe." I grabbed a cup out of the cupboard which was difficult to do when you had a muscled man attached to you. I poured coffee into the cup, adding two sugars and lots of milk.

"Here you go." I pushed the cup to the side of me. He didn't let go or move. "Uh, Mase, you need to unwrap yourself from me." I laughed. He shook his head and started kissing and nibbling on my neck. I let my head fall to the right, giving him more access, the scratch of his stubble sent heat straight to my core. I tried to wiggle out of his way which only caused my bum to grind into his manhood. I heard his breath catch in his throat.

"You may not want to do that." He pushed his hips forward and I could feel his hardness straining against his jeans. Shit, I felt awful. I was winding him up yet I couldn't help him release it either. How long would he wait for me?

I turned around in his arms, kissed him on the cheek and pushed him back with my hand on his chest. He looked at me confused, not moving too far away. The kitchen door opened and Ashlyn walked in. She was my closest friend now that Heather had left, the first time I met her was when we were both in the cold, dark, damp and smelly room at the Satan MC.

"Oh, sorry," she said as she went to walk away.

"No, it's ok. I was about to come and find you anyway," I told her. Mason took a step back from me, keeping his back to Ashlyn. He not so subtly rearranged his jeans and I had to try not to laugh.

"Oh, yeah? What about?" she asked as she walked into the room and poured herself some coffee. I hesitated, looking at Mason.

"What?" he asked, bringing the coffee up to his lips.

"Uh, girl talk." I nodded my head towards Ashlyn and he nodded. Kissed me quickly and left the room.

"What's going on?" Ashlyn asked as Drake and Solar walked into the kitchen. I saw her eyes lock onto Drake's and I had to nudge her to listen to me.

"Ladies." Solar smiled.

"What are you guys doing up so early? I didn't think the party finished til this morning?"

"Not been to sleep yet, sweetheart." Solar yawned, scratching a hand over his beard and grabbing the already made coffee that was in the pot.

"And yet you're having coffee?" I asked, eyebrows raised.

"Yeah, no time to sleep. We gotta ride in a minute."

"What? No, no you can't. That's too dangerous." I placed my hand on his arm so he would look at me.

"We live in a biker clubhouse, danger is all around us. Don't worry, sweetheart, I'll be fine." He palmed my face, smiling at me. I knew there was nothing sexual about the way Solar touched me, we had more of a brother/sister relationship and I surprised myself the most when I didn't flinch or shy away from his affection.

"We gotta... Get your motherfucking hands off my woman!" Mason yelled as he walked in as Solar's hand was on my face.

"Calm the fuck down, VP," he said as his hand fell from me. I wasn't doing anything wrong, was I?

"Cammie, a word," he bit out. I turned around to face him and all I saw was the kitchen door slamming shut.

"Sorry, Cam," Solar apologised.

"Don't worry. He's just over reacting." I pushed the door open, expecting Mason to be waiting for me and he wasn't. I walked down the long hallway and stopped outside of our bedroom, I took a deep breath and pushed the door open; I wasn't sure what I was going to be met with. I wasn't doing anything wrong. The room was empty and I was worried that he had gone off on his ride, mad with me. I wasn't going to see him for two days and I didn't want there to be any strain between us.

I quickly jogged down the hall, through the bar area and pushed the large door open, Mason was sitting on his bike, a cigarette hanging out of his mouth. Since when did he smoke? He looked up when he heard me, he jerked his head back, telling me to come to him. My feet didn't hesitate and before I knew it, I was in front of him, throwing my arms over his shoulders. He threw his cigarette on the floor, grabbed my hips and picked me up like I was a bag of feathers and placed me on his bike so I was straddling him. I tightened my hold around his neck, his smell calmed me, it was shower gel and now smoke.

"Hey, you ok?" he quietly asked in my ear as he ran his hand up and down my back.

"I though you left," I mumbled into his neck.

"Cam, look at me." I shook my head. "Cam?" I still didn't move and next thing I felt was him wrapping my blonde hair around his fist and pulling gently until my eyes met his.

"It didn't mean anything, Solar is like a brother to me," I rushed to say, I didn't want him to be angry at me or Solar.

"I know that, but it doesn't look good him touching what's mine," he growled. "If I let him do it, the others will think its ok too." My body froze after my mind registered his words. I didn't want anyone touching me apart from Mason. His touch soothed and calmed me.

"I'm sor..." My words were cut off when his mouth slammed onto mine and he pulled my body even closer to him. My body was starting to react differently to him, I would get hot, needy and I was sure my panties were starting to dampen. I hadn't reacted this way since before my time at the Satan MC. Sex was always a huge part of my life and I wanted that feeling back, that connection with Mason.

The sound of bikes revving up made me pull away from him. I looked over my shoulder and saw that Solar, Tat and Toes were waiting for him.

"Be good, Drake is going to look after you and Ashlyn. I'll see you in a couple of days." I climbed off his bike and started to move away when he grabbed my hand and placed something in it. I looked down at the phone, confused. "My number is programmed into it. I'll speak to you soon. I love you."

"Love you too, be safe. Please come home to me," I mumbled against his lips.

"See you soon, babe." After one last kiss, I stepped back and watched Mason put his helmet on, he started his bike, nodded his head at me and took off out of the compound.

Chapter 4

Mason

I had made it my mission to track down and find any remaining Satan's. They were a club that was full of bad blood. They gave the other clubs around here a bad rep. I had to fight with the rage that was in my chest so not to go out alone and kill every fucker that I came across. I needed to do this, I needed to get revenge for Cammie and I needed her to feel safe. I didn't want her worried or constantly looking over her shoulder. I wanted her to be able to go out when she wanted and not worry that she would be hurt, tortured or kidnapped. What about when we had a family? I wanted them all to be safe.

We all stopped as we pulled into the Pirates MC, the prospect recognised our cuts and let us straight in. The Pirates were based in the very south of Cornwall, their clubhouse backed straight onto a beach and several of them were keen surfers, they even went as far as printing the club patch onto their wetsuits.

"Holes," the Prez of the club greeted me. I pulled my helmet off and hooked it on the handlebar of my bike, climbed off my beloved black and chrome Harley Softail and shook his hand. "Prez."

"Come on in." We all followed him inside. Their clubhouse was an old B&B and as soon as you walked in you could smell the beach and the sea. There were several small rooms downstairs; a TV room with large leather sofas and a big ass flatscreen. The next room was a dining room, several tables and chairs were scattered around and there was a small hatch on one wall that opened up into the kitchen. The reception area was turned into a bar and that was where most of the Pirates were. The wall that led from the reception to a large living area was knocked down to make a bigger room.

"Holes," Horror greeted me, standing up and shaking my hand. He was a large guy, covered in tattoos and a bald head. He was named Horror as watching horror movies got his blood flow pumping.

"Horror, good to see you, man. How's it going being a VP?" We walked over to the bar and a small woman with bright red hair looked up at us.

"Two beers, Dixie." She nodded, turned around and bent down to the fridge, ass high up in the air. Her shorts were so short I thought her pussy was going to show. "Fancy a bit of that while you're here?" he asked, nodding towards the red head.

"Na, I got an Old Lady at home."

"Ah, she'll never know, man. That's the great thing about being a VP, all the ladies want us and they want to please us." Dixie placed the two bottles in front of us and gave me a wink. There was one thing for sure, my dick wasn't going near any female except for my Cammie.

Cammie

I was sitting at the bar sipping on a pear cider while Penny, the club bunny who was in charge of the bar, was wiping down tables, stocking the bar ready for the party tonight, which I would not be attending, not without Mason here and especially as I hadn't exactly accepted the leather cut yet.

"Hey, you ok?" Ashlyn asked as she sat on the bar stool beside me. I smiled weakly at her. "Penny, can I get a strawberry cider please?" Penny grabbed a cider for Ashlyn and passed it to her.

"Can we talk?" I asked.

"Sure, wanna go outside?" She knew that it would be more private, with no bunny ears listening in. I nodded and followed her outside, a few of the prospects and other club girls were hanging around the picnic benches, smoking. Ashlyn led me around the side of the clubhouse and towards the small park that was built for the Prez's kids.

"Where are you two going?" Drake questioned as he followed us.

"To sit on the swings and talk," Ashlyn replied. "Alone."

"Ok, I get it. Girl talk and all that. Just don't leave the club grounds. Mason will have my balls cut off and I'm quite attached to them." He winked at Ashlyn, laughing.

"We won't, I promise." He nodded his head and wandered away and we got comfy on the swings.

"Spill it," Ashlyn said before I even had a chance to talk.

"Is something going on between you and Drake?"

"What? No. Anyway we're talking about you, not me."
I took a deep breath and asked what I wanted to know.

"Have you, um... Had sex since the Satan's?" She shifted on the swing, took a long gulp from her bottle and looked at me. "Just once."

"Really? Here?" She nodded. "With who? How was it? Were you scared?"

"I was drunk, it was with one of the locals. Cory, you know the tall one, with the dark Mohawk. I was feeling lonely and needed to feel something. He was good, gentle. I kicked him out straight after we finished."

"Really?" I laughed, I never imagined Ashlyn to be a hit it and quit it kind of girl. "Do you regret it?"

"No, not really. I was glad that I didn't wait and did it, else the panic would have taken over. I just made sure he didn't pin me down, it was quick and I wasn't naked. I didn't want him to see..." Her voice caught in her throat and I knew she was talking about the scars on her body. Mine were bad enough but she had been there longer than me, she had twice as many. She was the one that told me not to scream, not to cry because they fed off that. She helped me in any way that she could, we bonded when we were in a horrible situation and I was so concerned for my own life that I didn't even know she left the Devon Destroyers clubhouse and disappeared.

"Have you and Mason not..."

"No, we've done stuff. He's not seen my scar." I placed my hand on my tummy, I could feel the ridges on my scar that the knife left through my thin t-shirt.

"Do you want to?"

"Yes, I really do. I love him and my body is slowly starting to come back to life. I'm just scared that I'll freak out on him."

"He loves you. He'll be gentle, considerate. You got the best of the bunch there." She smiled.

"Yeah, so nothing going on between you and Drake?" I asked again, hopeful of some gossip.

"Nope, he's hot. That's it." She shrugged her shoulders and finished off her drink.

"Come on, ladies, party is starting soon!" Drake called out. "The locals are coming in tonight." Just as he said that a tall guy with a dark Mohawk came up behind him. I nudged Ashlyn in the ribs and nodded towards the guys.

"Hey, Ash," Cory said. Drake turned around and glared at him.

"Hi, Cory." She smiled walking towards both men.

"Fancy a drink?" he offered. I nudged her again, I wanted her to be happy and he seemed like a nice enough guy.

"Sure." She walked past Drake and he didn't take his eyes off of her until she had disappeared into the clubhouse and was out of sight.

"You got it bad," I sung as I waked up to Drake.

He cleared his throat.

"What are you talking about?"

"You like her, don't you?" He placed his hand on my lower back and steered me into the clubhouse.

"Don't know what you mean, I appreciate a hot woman. Just like you."

"I wouldn't let Holes catch you saying that." Prez laughed as he walked out of his office.

"Just saying what I see, Prez."

"You know the club women are off limits," he reminded him.

"I'm just looking, no touching going on here. I'm glad it's locals' night tonight."

"Go and find one of the local girls to sink into, leave my girls alone." Drake saluted him and walked away, he grabbed the first local girl he came across and shoved his tongue down her throat.

"You need me to do anything tonight?" I asked the Prez.

"You don't work here, Cammie."

"Oh, I know that. I can serve at the bar, dance if you need me to?"

"No way, VP would go mad. Enjoy your night." He kissed the top of my head, much like I imagined a father would do and walked away.

Chapter 5

Mason

How you doing sexy? Mason
Hi, I'm missing you. You ok? Cammie
Yeah just havin some down time before the party tonight. Mason
Oh, there's a party? Cammie
Yeah. No need to worry sweet one. I'm all yours. Mason
Glad to hear it. I'm bored. Cammie
I'll keep you occupied when I get home. Mason
They won't let me work here. I need to get a proper job. Cammie
I stopped texting Cammie and hit the call button instead.

"Hello," she answered.

"What the fuck do you mean when you said 'they won't let me work here'?"

"No, Mason, not like that. I meant behind the bar, on stage or something."

"You are not getting up onto that fucking stage. You are my Old Lady, you do *not* dance. No one gets to see your body except for me." Well even I don't get to see it. I climbed off the bed and started pacing in the small room that was mine tonight. I needed to get home, I would have to leave and let the guys deal with the other club that was joining us tonight. We couldn't pass up on this chance of getting the info we needed. "I'll be home in a few hours," I bit out.

"No, Mason. Please stay and get what you need, I'm not working at the club. I'm in your room, in your bath tub, using Penny's bubble bath."

"Penny's? Why are you using Penny's? And now I want to be in that tub with you." There was silence on the other end of the phone and I had to check the display to see if we had been disconnected.

"Yeah, I had to borrow some from Penny as you didn't have any."

"That's because I don't use the tub, I shower." I pulled the phone away from my ear when I heard a beep. The front display read; New Message from Cammie. "Why are you sending me messages?" I opened the message just as she giggled on the end of the phone. "Shit." The picture was of Cammie in the tub, bubbles covering most of her. All I could see was her bright blue eyes, beaming smile and the tops of her glorious breasts.

"Did you like it?" she asked softly.

"Fuck yeah, I'll be using that picture later when I'm all frustrated thinking of you naked and in my bath tub."

"Mason!" She gasped.

Knock. Knock.

"Shit, babe. I gotta go. I'll call you later. Love you."

"Love you too."

I hung up the phone, slid it into my jeans and pulled the door open. Tat was standing in front of me. His hands were shoved inside his jeans pockets and he was rocking on his feet.

"They're here." I nodded, followed him out of my room and closing the door behind me. We walked to the large bar area, the Pirates MC were standing around the room staring at the small group of bikers that were leaning against the bar talking to the red head.

"Dixie, out!" Prez shouted. She did as she was told and quickly hurried away. I walked into the middle of the room and faced the VP from the Devils Descendants.

"Well, well. Look who it is. Holes." He nodded his head and I held out my hand for him to shake. He took it and we both sat down at the nearest table, my brothers standing behind me and his behind him. "What can we help you with?"

"I need everything you've got on the Satan MC."

He winced, running his hand over his face. He pressed his tattooed forearms onto the table and leant forwards. "What are you doing messing with a bunch of bikers like them?"

"They took something of mine and I want revenge."

"I heard your buddies from the Devon Destroyers took care of that."

"They thought they did, killed loads of them and burnt their clubhouse to the ground. There are more of them out there. I need to know where their new clubhouse is, rumours say they're in Cornwall."

"Sorry, can't help you."

"Bullshit!" I shouted, kicking my chair out from under me as I stood up in a rush.

"Holes," the Prez warned me.

"You wouldn't have travelled here to talk to me, on neutral ground to say you couldn't help."

The Pirates MC were known for trying to keep the peace, some say they are more laid back and relaxed because they are way out here with the sea and beach surrounding them. This is a clubhouse a lot of MC's come to when they needed neutral territory.

"What do I get in return?" he asked, folding his hands together on the table top as I looked down over him.

"What do you want?"

"A favour in return."

"What is it?"

"Don't know yet, but you have to do whatever I need you to."

"Holes," Tat said behind me. He didn't like what I was about to agree to.

"Done." I held out my hand and he shook it, I just made a

deal with the Devils. "Now, give me all the details. I want Intel on every Satan that's still alive."

"Tap." A shorter guy with blond hair stood up carrying his laptop. "Send everything you got to…" He stopped talking and looked at me. "Where do you want it sent?"

"Toes, give him the details. Thank you." I shook his hand and started to walk away.

"I'll be talking to you very soon."

I stormed out of the back door and was met with sand. I walked towards the sea and pulled my cigarettes out of my pocket; I had trouble lighting it as it was windy. I turned my back on the sea, cupped my hand around my fag and flicked the lighter. I breathed in a lung full of nicotine, this was the one thing apart from Cammie that calmed me.

"I don't know if that was the right thing to do, man," Tat said from behind me. I didn't acknowledge him, I didn't turn around. If this was his woman I'd like to see him deny her the protection she needed. The peace of mind it would give her to know they were well and truly gone.

"You don't know what shit he is gonna expect from you or how dangerous."

"Did we get what we needed?"

"Toes is just downloading all the details now."

"Then come back when you have information for me," I snapped. I needed time to think, I needed more information either from Cammie or Ashlyn. I needed to know what bastard took my girl and tortured her. He would be sorry he ever laid a finger on her.

Chapter 6

Cammie

I got out of bed early and started cleaning up after the party last night. I didn't attend, without him here, I didn't want to risk anyone thinking that I was a club whore. Drake was here to look after me and Ashlyn but I knew he would be busy working his way through the local women. The ones he was allowed to touch. Technically, Ashlyn wasn't property of the MC but they vowed to protect her so that meant Drake wasn't allowed to touch her either.

I was dumping all the empty bottles into a bin, cleaning down the sticky tables and trying to get the passed out bodies up. I was used to seeing naked people so it didn't bother me. I came across Titch, one of the newest prospects, he was short with long dark hair that touched his shoulders, tattoos covering just his arms and dark hair covering his chest. He was laid on the sofa with two girls either side of him. I nudged his foot with mine and his eyes popped open. His arms were crossed above his head and he raised an eyebrow at me, asking what I was doing.

"You need to get up, the guys will be back soon." He looked to both his sides, smiling. I'm sure he was remembering what had happened last night.

"Well, sweetheart, I need to sort that out first." He nodded to his manhood, which was fully erect. "So, unless you want to watch, I suggest you leave us in peace."

I stood in front of him, not really registering what he was saying. I only started moving away when he pulled the red head up over him and impaled her onto his cock. She let out a cry, throwing her head back. I turned around to leave and was almost knocked over by Daisy storming past me and out of the front door. Daisy was Heather's sister. She was also married to the last VP, Hitch, until he was killed. She didn't want to leave the club and no one seemed to know how well she was handling him being gone. She seemed fun and carefree when we first arrived, but now she was quiet, moody and was never usually around much.

"Am I in your way?" I called out after her. The noise of skin slapping together and moans had me leaving the bar and heading into the kitchen. I was surprised by the mess, it looks like someone wanted a late night snack. There was bread, butter and meat left out on the kitchen worktop. Tomato sauce was slowing dripping down over the side and onto the floor. At least this would keep me busy for a little while. I rolled up my sleeves and got stuck in.

"What you doing?" I heard behind me, making me jump. I looked over my shoulder to see Drake staring at me.

"Building a rocket." I rolled my eyes at him and he let out a loud laugh. "What a silly question, Drake."

"I meant, why are you cleaning?" He crossed his arms over his chest, making his dark t-shirt pull tight over his biceps.

"Because it's a mess." I turned back around and carried on with the job I set out to do.

"VP will be home soon, he won't be happy if he sees you in here cleaning."

I knew that Mason didn't want me working in the clubhouse, but I needed to do something to keep me busy. I was going stir crazy in here, I've never been one to sit back and let others run around after me. I needed to be active.

"Yeah, I know. I'm just about finished anyway." I put the cleaning supplies away and started making a batch of coffee.

"Here, I can do that." He took the jar of coffee out of my

hands.

"Drake, we're supposed to look after you guys..."

"The club bunnies are, not the Old Ladies."

"But, I'm not..."

"You are." He pulled a couple of mugs out of the cupboard above his head as I grabbed the milk out of the fridge. He finished making the coffees, adding sugar into mine. He passed me a cup and I smiled at him as I inhaled the smell of sweet aroma. One thing I couldn't live without was coffee.

"I'm going to enjoy this and catch up on the news," Drake said as he was about to leave the room.

"Um, Titch was in there and not alone."

"What the hell. I'm gonna move his scrawny, pale ass." He placed his hand on the door and as he pushed it open, he turned back towards me. "No more cleaning." I went to argue. "I mean it, Cammie." I nodded and took a small sip from my mug. Drake turned to walk away and stopped abruptly.

"Oh, hey VP." My head shot up and a smile covered my face as I saw the handsome face of my man. But he wasn't looking at Drake his eyes were burning into me, I couldn't read his expression, he wasn't smiling and he wasn't scowling. I took a step closer and Drake hurried away.

"I'm glad your home, I missed you." I placed my hand flat on his chest and stood up on my tiptoes and gave him a quick kiss on the lips. When he didn't return it I took a step back and finished off my coffee.

"Why have you been cleaning?"

"I was just cleaning up after the party, it kept me busy while waiting for you to come home..."

"You *do not* do the job of the club bunnies," he cut me off.

"Where the hell are they?" I shrugged my shoulders. I was up early, I didn't sleep well and I was too excited about seeing Mason today. He grabbed the empty mug out of my hand and placed it on the kitchen side. When he stood back up to his full height he placed his hands on my hips and guided me back against the wall. I never took my eyes off his pale blue ones, they were swimming with desire. Just that look alone had my underwear wet. I loved how my body reacted to him and I was ready to be with him completely. I wanted him to erase all the bad memories, I wanted to only feel his touch on me. I wanted him to own my body and soul.

"Cammie." His lips were close to my ear.

"Yes," I whispered.

"You do not clean. Ok?" His hands travelled up from my hips until they were touching the underside of my breasts. I nodded slowly, not taking my eyes off him. "Words, I want to hear the words."

"Yes," I whimpered. I wound my arms around his neck and pulled him in even closer so we were chest to chest. "Now, kiss me."

"Oh, I'm gonna do more than kiss you." He smirked and my eyes lit up. I wanted to feel him all over me; the heat from his skin, the roughness of his hands, the stubble from his face. He slammed his lips down onto mine and I immediately plunged my tongue into his mouth. I stood up on my tiptoes, trying to get closer to him. He knew what I was trying to do. He picked me up and I wound my legs around his waist, moving my body over the top of his. I needed to feel more of him. I let out a whimper and he pulled back.

"Don't stop," I pleaded.

"Not here." He took a step back and my feet landed on the floor. He pulled my hand into his and we headed for his room. I was surprised when we stopped a few doors away. Mason banged hard on the door, whose room was this? I was surprised when I saw a naked Lottie answering the door, yawning.

"Oh, hi, VP." She smiled, reaching up and fluffing her long dark, curly black hair which, in turn, caused her breasts to bounce.

"Get up, do your job or you'll be out. Got it?" he sneered at her.

"We've only been in bed for a couple of hours." She yawned.

"Not my problem, I will not have my Old Lady cleaning up when you four should be doing it."

"Old Lady?" she asked, sounding surprised. I pulled my hand out of Mason's and stood at the side of the door, I didn't really want to be standing there staring at her perfect body, she didn't have scars. Why would Mason want me, when he could be with someone like her? Someone flawless.

"Yes, she's my Old Lady, not that I have to answer myself to you. Get the other girls up and get this place looking as it should be."

He turned away from the door and looked at me, smiling.

"Now, where were we?"

I walked over to his door and pushed it open. I stood still in the middle of the room, not sure what to do. He wrapped his hands around me from behind and I heard the door slam shut. I quivered in his arms, I really wanted to be with him but maybe I'm not cut out to be in this lifestyle anymore. Maybe I needed a fresh start, on my own, in another country.

"What's running through that pretty little mind of yours?"

"Nothing." I spoke so quietly I don't know if he heard me. He spun me around to face him and his hands were on my hips again.

"What's going on?" I didn't answer him, I stared at his chest. I felt his hands move under my t-shirt and his right hand was dangerously close to my scar. He would be able to feel it. When he moved again I jumped back away from him. I could feel the tears running down my face, I tried to stop them but they just kept coming and coming.

"Hey, hey. What's all this?" He placed his hands on either side of my face and used his thumbs to wipe away my tears. It was no use they wouldn't stop falling.

"I think I should go," I whispered, stepping back from him again. I still couldn't bring myself to look him in the eye.

"Go?" he asked and I heard the word catch in his throat, I looked up and his eyes were full of worry. "You can't go, you can't leave me."

"I have to, I'm no good for you…"

"Stop that. Have I ever made you feel like you weren't good enough for me? That I wanted someone else? That I didn't love you?"

I shook my head. If I was completely honest with myself he made me happy, he made me smile and he made me feel like I finally belonged somewhere. That I was loved.

"Then why are you threatening to leave me? Don't you love me?" His fists were clenched at the side of his body. It wasn't because he was mad, it was because he wanted to touch me and I had backed away from him. He was trying not to push me too much.

"Mason, I do love you. I love you so much." I placed my hand over my heart. "This belongs to you and only you. But I don't think I can stay."

"I don't understand, I love you, you love me and yet you wanna run away?"

"I just… I… I'm… You have perfect girls out there, with hot bodies. Why would you want me when you can have them?"

"Why would I want them, when I only have eyes for you? You're mine, Cammie. I'm not letting you go." He crossed his arms over his chest.

"You'd keep me here against my will? Tie me up? Not let me leave? Just like they did!" I screamed the last bit.

"What? Fuck, no!" He stepped closer to me and pulled me up against his chest, he placed his lips on my neck and took some deep breaths. He did this when he was angry or upset, this seemed to calm him down.

"Do you see how much I need you?" His lips moved against my skin, his stubble scratching me. "You complete me."

A sob caught in my throat at his words, I needed him too. To chase away the bad dreams – I hadn't had one single nightmare since being with him. To help me forget the bad times, but in order to do that and move on I needed to tell him, no I needed to show him.

I took a step away from him and panic took over his face. I kissed him gently.

"I'm sorry..."

"No, Cammie, don't do this. Please?" He went to grab me again and I took his hand in mine and squeezed it.

"I'm sorry I haven't been honest with you. I love you so much Mason and being with you has made me the happiest I've ever been."

"Then..." I placed my finger on his lips to stop him talking.

"I'm trying really hard here. This isn't easy for me." I stopped talking and took a deep breathe. I let go of his hand, grabbed the edge of my t-shirt and pulled it over my head.

"Cam, you don't have to..." He stopped talking and his eyes zeroed in on my scar. "What's that?"

"I know, it's horrible. This is why I shouldn't be here, you can have any girl you want. One that isn't scarred."

He dropped to his knees in front of me and gently glided his fingers over it.

"When did this happen?"

I gulped, took a deep breath and spoke about the memories that I had tried to keep hidden for so long. "The Satan MC. They done that right before Blade came and rescued me, said it was a message not to mess with them."

"Who did this?" He stood up, picked me up and we curled up on the small sofa together. I didn't put my top back on, I needed to somehow be strong and find a way to bring my confidence back.

"They called him Switch. He was about six foot, dark hair, beard and tattoos covering him. He liked to... He liked to use his switchblade as he found his release. He was the clubs VP. Ashlyn was his favourite. He was always dragging her away and keeping her away for days."

"Was he the one who took you from the Devon clubhouse?"

"No, that was Preppy. He was very different from the rest of the guys. He wore his leather cut but he was always well dressed in trousers and polo shirts, he had slicked back blond hair and bright white teeth."

"Fuck, babe. I'm so sorry this happened to you."

"Yeah, but they were coming for Heather. I'm glad she didn't have to go through that."

"Can you tell me anymore?"

"Not today. I just want to feel you. Do you want me to leave?" I looked up at him.

"Fuck, no. I love you, baby. I want you here with me, I want you as my Old Lady. The full works." He smiled back at me. I stretched up so I could capture his lips in a kiss, it soon got heated and Mason pulled me into his lap, so I was straddling him. His hands were on my hips and as they began to explore my skin he touched over my scar and I shivered.

"Does it hurt?"

"No, it's a bit sensitive. I'm just not used to anyone touching it." I ran kisses over his jaw and down his neck. I pulled at the edge of his t-shirt, I wanted to feel his warm skin on mine. He sat up which caused us to be nose to nose which made me giggle.

"I love that sound, I will always promise to make you smile." He promised as he pulled his t-shirt off over his head and threw it onto the floor.

"And I promise to make sure you never need to look for another woman." I scooted back on his knees and popped the button open on his jeans.

"Cam, you don't have to."

"Oh, so you don't like having your cock sucked?" I had sunk to the floor in between his legs and looked up at him, my palms flat on his thighs.

"Fuck, I've been dreaming about those lips." I smiled and began pulling his jeans down, his hips rose off the sofa to help me. He wasn't wearing any boxers and he was rock hard. I gasped when I saw the piercings. I knew he was a piercer and that his lip, eyebrow, tongue and nipple was pierced, but I didn't know about these. I had never been with a guy who had his cock pierced before. I grabbed the bottom of his shaft and stroked upwards. I felt a barbell on the underside, he had one low on his cock by his balls and the same one the other side near his pelvis. I flicked the Prince Albert piercing on the top.

"Oh shit," he swore, laying his head back on the sofa. As my hand moved back down and gently over the piercings, I stuck out my tongue and played with the hoop in the tip of his cock. He was swearing, grunting and panting and I hadn't even taken him into my mouth fully yet.

"Take your bra off," he demanded. I reached around and unclipped my bra at the same time as I pulled him into my mouth. I wasn't sure how the piercings would feel and I was worried about hurting him. He glided in and out of my mouth easily, the two bottom piercings not making it into my mouth. I loved having control over him. I looked up at him and he was watching me. His hands were gripping onto the edge of the sofa so hard that his knuckles were turning white. I wondered if he was scared to touch me, in case he triggered a bad memory. This was one thing they never made me do. I knew that Mason loved to feel my hair when it was down and at the minute it was piled on top of my head again. I put it out of the way when I was cleaning. As I took him to the back of my throat again, I grabbed his right hand and placed it on my hair where my hair was tied up, I gave him an encouraging nod and he pulled the tie, causing my hair to fall around my shoulders. He tucked a piece behind my ear so he could see my face, my movements increased and his hold on my head tightened, I knew he was close. His chest was heaving up and down, a small line of sweat tricked down his forehead.

"Cam, you need to stop." I shook my head and palmed his balls with my free hand. I felt the first burst hit the back of my throat and I swallowed it down. I moaned at the taste, the vibration must have set him off as he swore, held my head still and filled my mouth with his release.

Chapter 7

Mason

It literally scared the shit out of me when Cammie told me she was leaving me a few days ago. I was glad that she had opened up to me, showed me her scar. To me it didn't change the way I felt about her, though it did give me more information to do what I set out to do.

Bang.

"Ok, church is in session!" the Prez called out after he slammed the gavel down. "First up, there has been some trouble down at 'Maze'. Tat and Solar, I want you to go down there and find out what the fuck has been going on. Brandon, the head bouncer was very vague on the phone."

"Sure thing," Solar answered.

"VP, you're up." Prez gave me the control of church.

"We had the meeting with the Devils, they gave us all of the info we were looking for and more information has become available. Toes, I need all the info you can get on Switch, the VP of the Satan's and some little shit called Preppy."

"On it." He didn't wait, he started tapping away on his laptop.

"What's the plan when it comes to the Satan's?" Drake asked.

"We don't rest until they are all dead. I want Switch for myself. No one else touches him, I want him alive." They all nod in agreement.

"Drake, make sure the girls have the bar full and ready for the party tonight. We have dancers coming in too. Make sure the stage is clear," the Prez ordered.

"Got it."

Prez slammed down the gavel and we all went about our business. As I left church, I looked around and saw Cammie in what looked like a heated discussion with Daisy. Daisy looked unsteady on her feet and Cammie looked like she was trying to hold her up. As I got closer, I heard some of the conversation.

"What is it exactly that you have been doing?" Cammie asked.

"None of your business," Daisy slurred.

"What's going on?" I asked as I stepped up beside Cammie. She looked relieved, like she welcomed the support.

"VP!" Daisy sung in her drunken state.

"Daisy, it's eleven in the morning, have you been drinking already?" I questioned her.

"No, I haven't stopped since last night." She smiled, pleased with herself.

"Ok, I think you need to sleep this off." I grabbed the top of her arm and began pulling her towards the bedrooms.

"Oh, am I gonna get lucky with the VP?"

"No, you're going to sleep," Cammie said as she pushed Daisy's bedroom door open. It was a complete mess, clothes everywhere, dirty cups and dishes on the floor. I pushed Daisy through the doorway and onto the bed, when I turned around Cammie had started picking up the dirty dishes.

"Leave that, she can sort her own mess out and if she's not careful she'll be homeless soon too."

"I'm just clearing away the dishes and mugs, they are starting to grow mould."

"Fine, give them here." She passed me the dishes and I threw them straight in the bin, grabbed the bin liner and walked out the door to chuck it in the outside bin. When I walked back into the clubhouse, I couldn't see Cammie. I went to check our room and as I walked past Daisy's room, Cammie was in there with her.

She was great with other people, she was kind, compassionate and mainly, she was all mine. A glimpse of our future popped into my head, Cammie sitting on the side of the bed of one of our sick children, reading to him, giving him medicine, being the mum I know she wants to be. Just seeing her with Heather and Blade's kids showed me how great she would be. She would be a natural and I couldn't wait until the day I'd feel our baby growing in her tummy.

"Hey, you ok?" Cammie asked as she stepped out of the room and quietly shutting the door behind her.

"Yeah. Let's go for a walk." She smiled and nodded her head. I took her out of the back door and led her down the steps to the beach. It was fairly quiet, with only one small shop and a lifeguard hut. With the weather warming up it would soon be busier.

"This is nice," she said as I wrapped my arm around her back; her blonde hair was blowing in the wind. She stopped and stood in front of me and tucked her arms around my waist underneath my cut, nuzzling her face against my chest, yawning.

"Tired, sweetheart?" She nodded, kissing my chest.

"Well, someone did wake me up early."

"Oh? And are you complaining about that?"

"No, it was a nice way to wake up. An orgasm is the best way to start the day." She laughed.

"It certainly is." I loved that Cammie now slept beside me naked, she wasn't as self-conscious about her scar and she had started using this special cream that helped it fade. I got the idea from Tat when I asked if he could cover it with a tattoo. He said that tattoos normally looked better when the scar was over a year old. It would be completely healed and not absorb the ink too much.

"Let's get an ice cream." She started pulling me towards the shop, she stopped before going in the door. "Oh."

"What's wrong?"

"It's shut, look." She pointed at a poster that said closed, position available. "Mason, I can work here. It says enquire at the lifeguard hut. Come on."

"Hold on." I pulled back on her arm, to stop her walking away.

"What?"

"You don't need to work, babe."

"I want to work, this place is perfect. It's close to the clubhouse. Please?"

"Let's at least see what they are offering, hours and pay."

"Thank you." She beamed up at me as she jumped into my arms and kissed the hell out of me.

"Well, it may have its perks, there looks like there is a back room." I winked at her and she giggled as I put her on her feet.

"Let's head over to the lifeguard hut and see if I can fill out an application." I loved seeing her smile and who knew that the prospect of a job would make her this happy.

Cammie pushed open the door to the hut and we couldn't see anyone.

"Hello?" she called out.

"Well hello." A young guy came walking out of the back room, long blond hair, wavy, I guess from being in the sea. He wasn't wearing a top and had on a pair of red board shorts.

"Hi, I'm Cammie." She held out her hand for a handshake and he shook it. "I've come to ask about the position available in the shop."

"Oh, have you now?" He looked her up and down and I took a step closer behind Cammie to let my presence known and to show him that she was mine. I placed my hands on her hips and kissed the side of her neck that was exposed from her hair. She smiled up at me and the guy cleared his throat.

"I'm Stuart, let me get Dan… Hey, Dan, there is a chick here about the job in the shop."

"Ideal!" Dan called back. He ran down some steps as Stuart ran up. I guess that was the lookout for the sea. Not that there was anyone in it.

"Hi, I'm Dan. Nice to meet you." He held his hand out for Cammie and then to me. That was polite, I respected him for that. Though I wasn't keen on the fact that neither of these guys seemed to own a t-shirt.

"Hi, I'm Cammie and this is M…"

"Holes, VP of the Cornish Crusaders," I cut Cammie off.

"Oh, yeah. I think I recognise you. Me and my mate Cory have been up to some of your parties. They're wild." He laughed.

"So, my girl wants some details on this job."

"Oh, sorry. At the minute, it's quite quiet so we only open four days a week, ten to four. In the summer, it's a lot busier and the shop will be open seven days a week, nine to seven, but we always get extra help in as that's a lot of hours for one person."

"Sounds great, can I get an application form?"

"No need, the job is yours if you want it?"

"Really? Yes, I'll take it."

"Great, let me just go through the days and how it runs. Take a seat." As he walked away, Cammie threw herself at me, wrapping her arms around my neck. I held her close to me and stood at my full height which caused her feet to come off the ground.

"You don't mind, do you?" she asked.

"I didn't realise I had a choice in the matter."

"If you really didn't want me working here, I won't. I want

you to be happy too."

"You can work here, on one condition."

"Oh yeah? Daily blowjobs?"

"You already do that, babe." I laughed. "You be my Old Lady…"

"I already…"

"Jacket and everything, it'll protect you. If people see you wearing that, they won't mess with you."

"I'll think about it." She kissed me quickly on the lips and I put her down once I heard Dan making his way back towards us.

"I'll be outside when you're done." I kissed her again and nodded my head towards Dan.

Once I was outside, I grabbed a cigarette and lit it. I tried not to smoke too much around Cammie, she already made it plainly clear that she hated it. I'd give up soon; one day.

Chapter 8

Cammie

It was party night and I put a little extra effort into my appearance. I was wearing a bright blue bodycon dress, it was low in the front and the entire back was covered in see through lace, stopping just above my bum. I paired it with some black heels, bright red lipstick and I curled my hair too. Mason and I still haven't slept together, we had gotten close several times and he had always stopped it, I think he was afraid that I wasn't ready and I was.

"Mmmm, you look sexy." I looked over my shoulder after I checked out my appearance in the mirror once more. Mason was leaning on the doorframe, his arms crossed over his chest and his t-shirt pulled in tight across his muscles, showing off his tribal half sleeve tattoo.

"You don't look bad yourself." I giggled.

He pushed off from the door frame and I thought he was headed straight towards me but instead, he walked past me at the last minute. I watched what he was doing and he went into the wardrobe. I thought he was going to change his clothes.

"Don't change, I love those jeans on you."

"Oh and whys that?"

"It shows off that ass well." I smiled, pinching it.

"Well, if you can't keep your hands off me, I'll never take them off." He winked at me and then carried on looking through his wardrobe.

"I much prefer what's underneath them," I whispered in his ear from behind. I didn't have to stretch too much as wearing my heels made me a bit taller. I stepped back when he tried to turn around.

"Here." I looked down at what he was giving me.

"Why are you giving me this?" I took the leather jacket from him.

"You're my Old Lady, you need to wear the properties." He simply shrugged his shoulders.

"I haven't agreed to that yet." I tried to give him back the jacket and he crossed his arms over his chest and stared at me. "I'm not taking it, Mason." I turned away from him and placed it on the bed.

"You need to wear it so everyone knows that you're mine."

"Well, everyone knows that I'm yours as this is only a club party tonight." I kissed him on his cheek and he held me closer as I began to move away.

"Why won't you wear it?"

"I will, just not tonight."

"You make me crazy, woman. You've turned me into a right pussy." He laughed, shaking his head and running his hand down his face.

"I hope I haven't as I'm all about the cock." I palmed him through his jeans and he growled at me. "Come on, let's go and get a drink and then you can do manly stuff, like shoot pool, drink shots and grope me on the dance floor." I winked at him as I walked towards the door, putting an extra swing in my hips.

***

The party was quite a quiet one, not one I was used to being around. Some guys were playing pool, some were playing poker and others were sitting around drinking. Me and Ashlyn were sitting at the bar talking.

"Why are the guys looking so miserable?" Ashlyn asked.

"No idea." I looked around until I caught Mason's eyes. He

was leaning over the pool table ready to take his shot. I swung around on my stool and crossed my legs, slowly, causing him to miss the ball. I couldn't help but giggle, he shook his head laughing to himself.

"Come on," I said to Ashlyn. We both grabbed our drinks and walked into the pool room. It was just off to the side of the bar and Mason was playing against Solar as Toes and Drake watched.

"Hey, baby." Mason smiled as I walked up to him and gave him a kiss.

"Holes, your turn," Solar grumbled. I took a step back and walked over to where Ashlyn was talking to Drake.

"I didn't say that!" Ashlyn bit out to him. They stopped talking once I was in earshot.

"Sorry, everything ok?" I asked.

"Yeah, Drake's just sulking as there are no locals here which means he can't get his dick wet."

"We're all pissed that there are no locals here." Solar added. "We need some more pussy, man." He slapped Mason on his back after he had taken his shot. "I've been waiting ages for my turn with Missy."

"You can't just expect her to go straight from one guy to the next. She's not a machine," I said looking at him.

"Maybe you couldn't in your whore days but I love it," Missy said walking in on the conversation and heading straight for Solar. She slipped her hand in his jeans and his smile increased.

"Hey, you don't talk to her like that. She's my Old Lady!" Mason barked.

"She's not wearing properties." Missy shrugged her shoulders and turned her attention back to Solar.

"She's my Old Lady and you all know that, don't give me that shit. Do you wanna be living somewhere else?" he threatened.

"Chill out, man, we don't have enough pussy here as it is. You're ok, you've got it on tap now," Solar said, nodding his head towards me.

"It's time to leave," Ashlyn said. I looked towards her and she nodded her head towards Missy, who was now on her knees and pulling Solar out of his jeans.

"Fuck!" Drake snarled as he stormed from the room.

I looped my arm into Ashlyn's as we walked out of the room and straight up to the bar. Drake was there talking quietly to Penny.

"You know I can't. I'll get kicked out and so will you." She smiled at him, placing her hand on his chest.

"You've got a hand, Drake, use it," Ashlyn spat before she walked away.

"What's her problem?" Drake asked me, looking confused.

"Desperation doesn't look good on you," I said before I turned away and went in search of Mason. I couldn't see him sitting with the guys playing poker and I knew he wouldn't be back in the pool room. I wondered if he was outside having a sneaky cigarette, I noticed that a lot of the time he tried to hide it from me, but I could smell it on him the majority of the time. As I headed towards the front door, I felt a hand grab my wrist, I yelped in surprise. I wasn't scared, I knew as soon as the electricity zapped through my body that it was Mason that had grabbed me.

"Where you going?" he asked into my hair as he pulled me up against his body, my back to his front.

"I was looking for you. I thought that maybe you were having a sneaky smoke."

"Me? No, whatever gave you that idea?" He laughed.

I turned around in his arms and looked at him, eyebrows raised.

"Ok, you got me. I went back to our room for my cigarettes." He showed me the pack.

"Now, the question is, can I tempt you away from them?" I asked quietly in his ear, dragging my lips slowly down his neck.

"I'm sure you can find a way." His breathing was laboured and I could feel his excitement in his jeans, pressing against my tummy. I pushed him flat against the wall and he watched as I trailed my finger down his body, from his throat, over his chest and abs until I stopped at the top of his jeans. His eyes were burning into mine, pale blue eyes into bright blue ones. Though his were turning darker every time I got closer and closer to touching him. I slipped my hand inside his jeans and grabbed a hold of him. He hissed between his teeth and I reached up so my mouth was close to his ear again.

"I want this." I squeezed him again. "Inside of me."

Mason

Fuck, what was she doing to me, I never let a woman have this much power over me before but on Cammie it was sexy as hell. I loved how each day I saw more and more confidence in her.

"You want me inside of you, babe?" I spoke softly. Her eyes met mine, she bit her bottom lip and nodded her head. "Once you're wearing my property jacket, you can have as much of me as you like."

Her head snapped back, looking at me shocked. "That's not fair," she complained.

"Come on, Cam, I don't see what the big deal is. It's just a jacket, I'm not asking you to marry me."

"You may as well be, it's just as much of a commitment." She released me from her hand and took a step back. I missed the warmth her hand gave me, but my hard on didn't soften.

"I want to make love to you, as my Old Lady."

She took a step closer to me and I thought that I had won her over.

"Then fuck me, Mason." I groaned inside, not letting her know that she was getting to me. What was wrong with me? There was a sexy as fuck woman, who I was in love with, standing in front of me asking me to fuck her and I wasn't doing anything about it, why? My resolve faltered and I slammed my lips down onto hers, my hands going straight for her hair. She moaned and her hips bucked into mine. Fuck she was hot. I tried to slow down the kiss, releasing her hair and letting my hands roam down her back until they found her ass. She moaned into my mouth again as she licked and nipped at me. I could feel her trying to get her body as close to mine as possible. I picked her up and her legs wound around my waist, I turned us and slammed her into the wall. She used her feet to lock her legs around my back and she began to rub herself all over my hardness. I could tell she was getting close to a release as her breathing changed and she stopped kissing me. I pulled away.

"Mason!" she complained.

"Not here, no one apart from me in this clubhouse will hear you come." She nodded frantically as she unhooked her feet and let her legs drop down to the floor. I grabbed her hand and we practically ran to our room. Once we were inside the door, she grabbed the bottom of her dress and pulled it straight over her head showing me that she wasn't wearing a bra and underwear that wasn't really covering a lot. I slipped off my leather cut placing it onto the small sofa, not taking my eyes off my beautiful woman. I reached behind me and dragged my t-shirt off over my head. Her eyes sparkled with lust, twinkling with desire. I was really going to enjoy this. I stalked towards her and wound one hand around the back of her neck keeping her close to me and the other on her lower back, her skin was soft and warm and I wanted to feel other places.

I started walking forwards, causing her to walk back and as soon as her legs hit the bed we were falling and I was completely on top of her, I was slightly worried she was going to freak out but she just pulled me closer.

"I love feeling you on top of me, caging me in. Making me yours." She spread her legs causing me to fall against her wet spot, even through my jeans I could feel the heat radiating off of her. It would be difficult not to just spread her legs and plough into her like I so desperately wanted to do.

"Mason, please," she begged, running her nails up and down my bare back. I was lavishing her in kisses, I wanted to taste every part of her. I worked my way down her body, stopping when I reached her panties. I looked up to her and she rose her hips off the bed in invitation. I ripped them off her body and spread her legs wide, using my hands to hold her open to me. I lowered my head until I knew she could feel my breath over her pussy.

"Is this what you want?" I asked.

"Yes, please, Mason. Yes!" She squirmed on the bed and I pinned her legs still as I dragged my tongue through her folds, she let out a long relieved sigh, her eyes fluttering closed.

I licked, nipped and rubbed her, bringing her close to orgasm, several times she had tried to move her legs to wrap them around my head. I knew this was the best way for her to come but I kept her legs pinned to the bed, she wouldn't be coming that easy.

"Mason, I need..." she panted.

"What do you need, baby?"

"I need you to either fuck me with your cock or let me wrap my legs around your head."

I didn't do either, I just kept torturing her that little bit more. Loving the way her pussy got wetter and wetter for me. Seeing her opened up for me took every ounce of willpower I had not to slam into her. The first time she came around me, milking me, strangling the head of my cock, she would indeed be my Old Lady.

"Babe, please," she begged. I stopped and looked up at her. Her face was red, she had a glistening sheen of sweat on her chest and her hands were fisted into the sheets by the side of her.

I glided my tongue once more through her folds and once I landed on her clit, I released the hold I had of her and she immediately wrapped her legs around my head and began thrusting her hips up. My tongue was on her clit and she used my chin to grind against, it was so hot and I was painfully hard. I loosened my jeans as she lost herself trying to find her release. Just seeing the look on her face would have me coming in my jeans. I squeezed myself and when I could feel her about to come I began to furiously pump my cock in my hand. Within seconds, she screamed out in pleasure and her legs instantly loosened. I jumped to my feet and her head rose off the bed, watching what I was doing. My hand moved faster and faster as hot jets started shooting out of my cock, all over her tummy and pussy. Now she was truly claimed by me.

"You made a mess." She laughed.

"Better here, than in my jeans." I smiled. I rubbed my release over her pussy and she gasped in surprise.

"Now you can't fuck me." She sulked. I looked at my cock and he was already stirring to life, she followed my line of vision. "Oh, maybe you can." She smiled.

"Wasn't going to anyway, sweetheart." Her face dropped and I couldn't help but laugh. "Come on, let's get you cleaned off." I grabbed her hand and pulled her to her feet and we ran for the bathroom before we made any more mess.

Chapter 9

Mason

"What the fuck is going on?" I heard the Prez shout as I got closer to the bar area. When I rounded the corner, I saw about fifteen women lined up against the bar. I stopped by Prez's side, waiting to hear what was happening.

"We're interviewing," Toes said grinning.

"What the hell for?"

"Club bunnies." Toes said it like that was a silly question.

"We don't need no more girls around here, creating trouble," he fumed.

"There isn't enough pussy to go around here anymore," Tat piped in.

"Why don't you put in the fucking effort and go out and find your own pussy," he yelled.

"Mike?" Carla said worriedly from behind him. I looked over my shoulder and saw that Cammie was standing beside her looking at all the women that were in the room.

"It's ok, babe," he said to her. "Just these guys being total dicks." He turned back to Toes. "Get them out of here, I don't want to see this again."

Toes nodded. "Some of them had such sexy feet too," he grumbled whilst walking over to the women. Toes got his name as he loved to suck on his conquests toes as he fucked them, disgusting if you ask me, but whatever floats his boat.

After all the women were escorted out, some of them complaining and pouting about it, Toes and Tat joined me, Cammie, Drake, Solar and Titch at a table while Missy got us some coffee.

"I think a trip to club orange is called for," Tat announced.

"Oooo, clubbing? I want to come," Cammie squealed excitedly. The guys laughed and she looked at them confused.

"We're on a pussy finding mission," Solar told her.

"When are you not? I wanna dance with my sexy man." She smiled up to me, kissing me briefly on the lips.

"If my woman wants to go, then we're going too." The guys groaned.

"Hey, I can help," she complained, slapping Solar on the arm.

"Oh yeah and how are you going to do that?" Toes asked.

"By showing everyone there that the most gorgeous biker is taken." She beamed and snuggled in to me.

"No way is he the gorgeous one, have you seen all these tats?" Tat asked, showing off his arms.

"And look at this strong jaw line, and perfectly trimmed beard?" Solar said stroking his hand across his jaw.

"And this." Toes stood up and grabbed his jean covered dick in his hand. "Makes me the most gorgeous of all," Toes bragged.

"Is it pierced?" Cammie asked. Toes' faced paled.

"Um..." He looked at me and I shrugged my shoulders. "No."

"Then it's not the most gorgeous one at this table." She crossed her arms over her chest, trying to hold in her laughter.

"Is that what women like these days? Pierced junk?" Solar asked, resting his elbow on the table.

"Oh the pleasure." She smiled, winking at them.

"Fuck me. Holes can you pierce me?" Toes asked.

"Are you serious? She tells you that one thing and you want it pierced? What about healing time, man," Tat said.

"Oh yeah, can I not fuck after having it done?" Toes looks at me.

"Sex is normally fine after about two to three weeks, but you have to be gentle and wear a condom. Normal healing time is four to six weeks," I informed him.

"Fuck it, let's do it," Toes announced, standing up.

"Maybe you should get a pussy fix first, what if it takes six weeks to heal, man?" Titch added.

"Yeah, good plan. Club Orange? Up for it? Tonight?" Toes asked, looking around at us all.

"Yes!" Cammie called out. "I'm going to tell Ashlyn." She stood up from the table. "Is it local?"

"Kind of, it's in Devon. Fresh pussy!" Toes called out, high fiving everyone except me.

"Ok, cool." She kissed me on the lips quickly before hurrying away.

"You've got one cool woman there, dude," Tat said, slapping me on the back.

"And she's smokin too," Titch added looking in the direction she went. My hands were clenched into fists and I was breathing deeply trying to control myself to not knock the fucker off his feet.

"Uh, Holes? How about you go and tell the girls we'll be leaving in a couple hours?" Solar said, nudging me off my seat. I looked at him and nodded. I turned around to walk away and I saw Drake pulling Titch out of the clubhouse. I'm hoping it was to give him a talking to. Most guys would love the fact that other men lust after their women, but not me. They need to keep their eyes, hands and thoughts to themselves.

Chapter 10

Cammie

We were headed for club orange in Devon. The name sounded familiar but I couldn't remember if it was somewhere that I had been before. I called Heather to see if her and Blade could meet us but she said as it was so short notice that they didn't have time to get a babysitter and that she would come and see us very soon. I hoped she would as I missed her.

We stepped off the rented bus that Titch had been nominated to drive and headed inside the club. It was big and bright, all the furniture was in orange, I guess that's where the name came from and there was something familiar about the place. Mason held onto my hand as we walked up to the bar, he was looking hot in his dark denim jeans, biker boots, black shirt and his leather jacket. Did he always go everywhere wearing that thing?

"What do you want, baby?" he shouted over to me.

"Vodka and orange please." I smiled. His eyebrows rose in question. "Well, we are at club orange." I laughed.

He leant over the bar shouting our drink order to the bar maid. When he got close to her ear, she smiled and bit her bottom lip, I bet I knew exactly how she was feeling, hot, wet and thinking she would be getting lucky with him. When she turned away to make our drinks, I pushed myself in between him and the bar, using the small step to stand on to make myself taller.

"Hey, sexy lady." He smiled.

"Hi, hot stuff. Can I get your phone number?" I joked.

"You can have anything you want." He placed his hands on

my hips, took a step back and his gaze swept my body. He had done this several times tonight. "You're looking so sexy, I don't know how I'll be able to control myself." I was wearing a short black skater dress with a low rounded neck line and I had on my heeled biker boots and my usual bright red lips.

"I don't want you to control yourself." I winked at him before I grabbed his leather jacket in both hands and pulled him close so I could plant my lips onto his.

"Oh, um… Here are your drinks." The bar maid said, causing us to break apart. Mason handed her some money and told her to keep the change. She beamed at him, her eyes full of desire and his eyes never left mine. She clearly thought she was in with a chance even though moments before she interrupted us his tongue was down my throat. I was never one to get jealous, not since being a sweet bun at the Devon Destroyers MC. They rescued me when I needed it the most, when I was broken and lost. I was at the point in my life when I didn't care, I didn't care what happened to me, I let them all use my body, it was the only way I could get myself to feel. I was numb to everything else. I didn't have any friends, no one I cared about and no one cared about me. Not until Heather had joined us, she was like a big sister to me with the seven year age gap. She cared for me and in return I tried to help her in any way that I could.

"Have you been here before?" Ashlyn asked me, standing next to me at the bar. Drake followed her and I remember Mason saying that the Prez said Drake had to look after her tonight, with the way he was looking at her I didn't think he would think it was a hardship. He looked like he was enjoying himself.

"I don't know, something seems familiar about this place."

"It used to be called club zero about a year ago."

That was it, I knew I had been here before. How could I have forgotten this place?

"Hey, sexy, you wanna dance?" I had just turned eighteen and I was fed up of my life, I was falling into a pit of despair after going through a year of hell. I needed to feel something, anything, that's why I came out tonight on my own in an extremely short dress and a face full of make-up. I wanted to have fun, I would never fall in love again and I would never put myself through the pain of losing another child.

"Sure," I answered, downing the last drop of my vodka and coke and shooting back the tequila slammer someone had brought me. He held my hand and led me into the middle of the dance floor and pulled me in close to him. He was handsome, with short blond hair, fitted jeans and a striped shirt. He had some tattoos on his forearms and I could see one peeking out the top of his shirt.

"How old are you?" he whispered closely to my ear, pulling me in so we were now chest to chest.

"Twenty. It's my birthday," I lied.

"Oh really?" He smirked. *"And what does a pretty thing like you want for her birthday?"*

"To feel," I mumbled to myself.

"What was that?"

"Um, whatever you want to give to me." I smiled sassily at him. I realised I sounded like a complete whore but at this point in my life, I just didn't care. I wouldn't have cared if I got hit by a bus tomorrow, at least I would have been with Noah again. My chest constricted and I felt a panic attack coming on. I needed a distraction. I grabbed the back of, whatever he was called, head and pressed my lips to his. He quickly invaded my mouth with his tongue and I felt disappointed that I didn't feel anything. I was just going through the motions. After a couple of minutes, we broke apart and he placed his forehead against mine.

"Fuck, babe. You've made me hard."

Could I go through with sleeping with him even though I didn't feel anything?

"I need a drink." He nodded, grabbed my hand and pulled me to the bar. As we were waiting to be served, I noticed a group of guys walking in the door, they were all in leather jackets and they had a look about them, a not to be messed with look. That was a complete turn on and I couldn't stop staring at them. One of them caught my eye, he was tall, dark haired and led the group of guys to the bar. Once they turned around to order drinks, I saw that on the back of their leather jackets there was a symbol and the writing said 'Devon Destroyers MC'.

"Here you go, babe."

"July, my name is July."

"Jay, that's the name you'll be screaming later." He chuckled and I looked down to see that he had passed me a bottle of some blue coloured shit.

"What's this?"

"Alcohol." He laughed. "Drink up."

I placed the bottle back onto the bar. "I don't think so." I waved to the bar man and asked for a vodka and coke and a shot of anything.

"It's not nice to refuse my drink," Jay growled into my ear and for the first time tonight, I felt something, I felt fear.

"I can't mix my drinks. I'll be sick later if I do," I explained, looking at him and hoping that I wasn't making him angry. Over his shoulder, I saw the guy from earlier. He was leaning against the bar, one foot crossed in front of the other and he was watching me, watching us. He held a bottle in his hand and he looked hot. I wanted to dump this guy and go introduce myself, there was something about him that called out to me.

"Let's dance," he said grabbing hold of my elbow.

"I'm getting tired, I may head home in a minute."

"You're going to dance with me, you aren't getting away that easily after teasing me with this body of yours." He ran his hand down my back until it landed on my bum. What had I gotten myself into? He dragged me onto the dance floor, placed my back to his front and started dancing, he wound his arm around my stomach holding me close to him.

"Move those hips of yours, July," he growled into my ear and I obeyed him. We were still facing the bar and that guy's gaze still hadn't left mine. Would I be able to mouth that I needed help? Would he help me?

After a few more songs, my feet were killing me, I needed to sit down so I made up the excuse that I needed the toilet. Maybe there would be a window I could escape through. No such luck, there was only one window and I would be lucky if I could get my arm through it, let alone anything else. I had been away from him for ten minutes, I knew I needed to go back. If he was distracted, I'd try and sneak away from him. When I rounded the corner that led back to the bar, I saw the biker guy standing in front of Jay, was this my chance to escape? Before I could think anymore, the biker guy's eyes were on me and he nodded me to come closer. My feet were moving on their own accord and before I knew it, I was standing in front of him.

"Sweetheart, is this your boyfriend?" he asked. I shook my head. "You going home with him tonight?" I shook my head again. "Good." He pulled his arm back and punched Jay straight in the face. I squealed and took a step back, my head spun around when I felt a pair of hands on my hips. This guy was tall and skinny and wearing the same leather jacket as the other guy. What was going on?

"Let this be a lesson to you!" the guy shouted at Jay as he took a step back.

"Ripped!" the guy behind me called out as his hold on me loosened. Ripped took a step closer to me.

"He put a date rape drug in your drink." I think he saw the look in my eye. "In the bottle you didn't touch." Relief flooded me.

"Thank you."

"I think its best that you go home."

"Let me at least buy you a drink to say thank you?" I asked.

"No woman is buying me a drink," he growled, taking a step closer to me, I didn't back away. "But I'll buy you one, if you want to hang *out with us." I nodded my head furiously. Just one look from this guy had me feeling things and I was determined to feel more.*

That was how I ended up being a sweet bun at the Devon Destroyers clubhouse, they gave me a place to stay and food on the table and all I had to do was spread my legs and dance. I wasn't worthy of anything else, not after failing as a parent and letting my son die.

Mason

Cammie spaced out for a few minutes and she had a lost look in her eyes, I had tried so hard over the last few months to rid that look from her face, I thought I was succeeding but something had put that look back there.

"Come and dance with me," I said as I grabbed hold of her hand and squeezed it gently until she looked at me. Once her bright blue eyes connected with mine, the lost look disappeared and she nodded.

The dance floor was crowded with people and I pulled Cammie in as close to me as possible. We started swaying to the music and she wrapped her hands around my neck and mine were on her hips.

She pulled away from me slightly and looked me in the eye.

"I'm so in love with you, Mason." The grin that erupted on my face was the biggest one I've ever had.

"I'm very much in love with you too. Will you wear my properties?" She was probably fed up of me always going on about it but I wanted her to wear it and show everyone she was mine, at least until I could get a ring on her finger.

"How could I possibly agree to wear your jacket when I don't know how good you are in bed?" She was trying to keep a straight face but I could see her lips twitching as she tried not to laugh.

"Oh, baby, I'll show you how good I am in bed. In the shower. Against the wall. On my bike." I winked at her.

"Show me and if I'm completely satisfied, I'll wear your properties."

"That sounds like a challenge?" She shrugged her shoulders at me, smiling. "One I am very happy to accept. Let's go home."

"We can't. We haven't even been here an hour and all the guys look busy." I glanced around and saw that Solar, Toes, Tat and Titch all had a woman with them. Drake was dancing with Ashlyn, which was something I had to keep an eye on. He wasn't allowed to touch club women, not until he was patched in.

"What's going on there?" I asked Cammie as I nodded towards Drake and Ashlyn.

"Nothing. I asked her about it as they seemed close at one point. She has been seeing one of the local guys and lately all those two do is bicker and snipe at each other."

"Keep an eye on her for me, I'd hate to have to kick her and Drake out. He's gonna be a great member."

"When does he patch in?"

"When Prez says so. It's normally around the year mark or if he earns it some other way." She nodded and looked at them again.

The beat of the song increased and we both moved our hips in time, my hands had left her hips and were caressing her back, making their way towards her delectable ass. I dipped my head closer to her ear.

"Are you wet for me?" Her breath hitched in her throat and she nodded her head. "How wet?"

"Soaked. I need you, Mason. So bad."

"Ah fuck, don't tell me that. You said we can't leave," I groaned.

"We can find a dark corner somewhere, though I can't promise I'll be quiet," she said as she rained kisses over my neck, sending pleasurable sensations flowing throughout my body.

"No. The first time will be in our bed. Where I can take my time."

"Mmmm, I'm definitely going to enjoy this." She smiled at me, her eyes dancing with excitement.

"Oh, I can guarantee it." I cupped her face in my hands, tilted her head until I could devour her lips. They were always soft and inviting. I didn't know what I had done to deserve her but, one thing I knew, I was never letting her go.

Chapter 11

Cammie

Mason didn't waste any time getting us home and the bus was fuller with Toes and Solar bringing women with them. Did they tell them we were heading into Cornwall?

As soon as the bus came to a stop, Mason took hold of my hand and we quickly walked to our room. Once the door closed and locked, Mason stared at me.

"Are you sure?"

"Yes," I whispered, unable to do or say much more as my body was on edge. Mason had touched and kissed every bare bit of skin that was available to him in the club and I was pretty sure I was going to go off like a rocket as soon as he touched me properly.

He slowly walked towards me and I kicked my boots off. His hands palmed my face and he kissed me gently, my hands instinctively went to his arms and I felt him shiver from my touch. The kiss started to deepen and I stretched up on my tiptoes to get closer to him. My hands had found their way underneath his shirt and I held onto his sides. His left hand slipped from my face to the top of my dress where he unclipped the button and slowly pulled down the zip, the cool air hit my back and my nipples instantly hardened. This dress had a built in bra so there was no need for one. He pushed the dress off my shoulders exposing my breasts and I found my way to the buttons on his shirt, quickly undoing them. He had already taken off his leather jacket throwing it onto the dressing table.

We both made quick work of getting each other naked and

Mason picked me up and placed me gently in the middle of the bed.

"Please don't wait, you teased me loads at the club and on the bus ride home," I said, breathlessly.

"The first time is going to be fast." I nodded. "Do I need a condom?" I nodded again and he swore as he searched his bedside table for protection.

Once he was protected, his body came into contact with mine and I shivered.

"You ok?" I nodded. No words would come out, my body was buzzing with excitement and I couldn't wait for us to be connected together. He was laying over the top of me, holding himself up with his arms. I placed my hand on the back of his neck.

"I need to feel you, the weight of you on my body." He loosened his arms and gently lowered himself until we were touching skin on skin. My hardened nipples pressed into his hard muscles. Our lips began their dance again and I placed my hands on his face, loving how he made me feel. I could feel him at my entrance and I rose my hips off the bed telling him I was ok. He slowly pushed inside of me as his tongue invaded my mouth, our kisses turned fast and frantic and I gasped when he was completely inside of me. His barbell piercing was pressed against my clit and he slowly withdrew just a little and pushed back in again, showing me that his piercing would hit my clit each time. That was hot. He started a steady rhythm as he kissed down the side of my neck, he was using his forearms to keep himself up.

My hands were exploring his skin, I loved feeling his muscles as he worked himself in and out of me.

My skin was hot, I could feel a sheen of sweat covering us both and we were both panting with the need for a release.

"Mason!" I gasped as he sped up. I could feel his Prince

Albert piercing inside me and along with the barbell torturing my clit it wouldn't be long until I exploded.

"Come for me, Cammie," he demanded in my ear, rubbing his thumb over my nipple.

"Yes," I told him breathlessly. I could feel it, the build-up in my lower spine, my face felt flushed, my legs were caging him against me and my nails dug into his back as I screamed out. I could feel myself pulsing around him as his hips accelerated and continued to pound into me.

"Tell me your mine."

"I'm yours."

"Tell me you'll be my Old Lady."

"Mason!" I cried out again as an unexpected orgasm hit me. "I'll be your… Old Lady."

"Cammie!" he called out as his hips stopped moving at their fast pace and leisurely moved in and out of me until he collapsed on top of me completely.

"I love you," I whispered in his ear.

"You too," he mumbled into my neck, which caused me to giggle. He pushed himself up onto his hands which caused me to gasp as he was still semi erect and inside of me. He frowned, his way of asking what was funny.

"You mumbling into my neck because you were too tired to talk properly."

"I've wanted that for so long, I think I blacked out for a minute." He smiled at me, brushing the hair off my face. "I need to sort this condom out before it decides to split." My eyes widened and he must have noticed. "Don't worry, we'll get you on the pill soon until we're ready to start a family." He kissed me quickly on the lips and walked into the bathroom.

Ready to start a family? I was in full panic mode, I've only just got Mason and now I was going to lose him. When I told him that I couldn't have a family with him, that I was too scared to carry another baby, what if the same thing happened again? I wouldn't survive losing another child.

I pulled the duvet up and over my naked body, I laid on my side away from Mason so he couldn't see my tears. When I heard the bathroom door open, I faked sleep so I wouldn't have to explain anything to him. The bed dipped when he climbed in beside me.

"Cam?" he whispered, placing his hand on my arm. I stayed still as he laid down and pulled me in against him, burying his face into my neck. "I love you," he quietly said before his breathing evened out and he was asleep.

Chapter 12

Mason

I was waiting on Cammie to finish getting ready, I'd woken her up by kissing and nibbling all over her body. When she finally woke up, she pushed me to the bed and rode me until we both screamed in pleasure. If this was how it was going to be between us, I needed to pop out and get some more protection today.

I was excited to show Cammie off as my Old Lady and knew that the Prez would instigate a party to celebrate.

"You ready, Cam?" I called out just as the bathroom door opened and she walked out in a pair of tightly fitted skinny jeans, her biker boots from last night and a long flowy top that had a dip in the cleavage.

"Shit, you look hot." I appraised her from her to toe while licking my lips before asking, "Wanna go for a ride later?"

"I thought that's what I did this morning." She smiled as she wrapped her hands around my neck and pulled me down to kiss her. I placed my hands on her ribcage to stop us falling back onto the bed.

"Come on, let's get some breakfast, I'm starving," I told her pulling away and handing her the leather jacket that was now hers.

"Uh, Mase, it's two in the afternoon, breakfast was hours ago." She slipped the jacket on and pulled her hair out from under the collar.

"Late lunch then. That looks good on you." She smiled at me and we left our room hand in hand and entered into the busy bar. Why was there so many people around?

We stood by the bar and I turned to face everyone, pushed my fingers into my mouth and whistled. The room fell silent.

"Everyone, I'd like to introduce my Old Lady, Cammie." There was some whooping and cheers and Ashlyn had flung her arms around Cammie and they were talking so fast I couldn't keep up.

"You know what this means? Party tonight!" Prez called out. "Congratulations, VP." he said, shaking my hand.

"With locals, Prez?" Toes asked.

"Yes and dancers if you wanna be in charge of sorting it out?"

"Hell yeah," he agreed. "What time?"

"Let's start now. Two whiskeys please, Missy." Prez ordered two drinks and placed one down beside me as Ashlyn dragged Cammie away. I made sure to know where she was at all times, she was now the most important person in my life.

Cammie

The party had been flowing for the last few hours and I was starting to get a little tipsy. I was sitting at a table with Ashlyn and Cory and he had brought his friend Dan, which was a little awkward as he was my boss. I was starting my new job in a couple of days and I didn't want to give off a bad impression.

"What the hell is that noise?" I complained. It sounded like an alarm. Were we being invaded? My eyes shot around the room looking for Mason and he was playing pool, he didn't seem concerned so neither was I.

"Shit, that's my car alarm," Toes announced as he dashed outside. "What the fuck!" he roared.

I jumped to my feet and ran outside to see what was going on and there was a young woman, with long dark hair, pale skin and in a small dress. Was she the girl he brought back with him last night? What was she still doing here? She was standing by his car with a baseball bat in her hand. She had smashed all the windows and lights on Toes car.

"What the fuck do you think you're doing?" he shouted at her, causing her to flinch.

"You," she said pointing the bat at him. "Brought me here, with you. We had a fantastic night and then I find you all over some other girl."

Toes began to laugh. "Steffi, that's what being a club whore is all about, you have to share me and I'll share you."

She paled. "A club whore?" She sounded confused. "I don't understand."

"I brought you here to pleasure us. You can stay as long as you continue to do so." He turned towards the other club brothers. "Can you believe this, she thought she was getting a boyfriend." He laughed and they all joined in.

Steffi had sunk against the wall, the bat fell out of her hand and she looked scared.

"Stop it. All of you!" I snapped. I know I wasn't meant to talk to club members this way, but they were being disrespectful. "She's still a person. She's not a piece of meat, and you." I pointed at Toes. "Please tell me you didn't lead her on? Tell me that you explained how it all works here."

"I'm in a leather cut for Christ sake. If she didn't know then she's stupid."

"Not everyone is out looking for a club whore!" I shouted. "And not everyone knows how a place like this works. I didn't until it was explained to me."

Everyone stayed quiet and no one spoke, I was waiting to be told off. I looked at Mason and he was smiling at me, he looked proud to know that I stood up to them. I walked quickly towards Steffi and she backed away from me.

"I'm not going to hurt you. Come with me and we'll get you cleaned up." She nodded and as we started walking past everyone, I looked at Mason.

"I think you need to teach these pigs some lessons in being a real man."

"Fuck," he swore. "I just fell even more in love with you!" he called out after me.

Once we were in my room, I showed her the bathroom and gave her a change of clothes.

"Do you want to come out and find me? Or shall I wait here?"

"Would you mind waiting?"

"Of course, I'll wait." I sat back against the headboard and picked up my kindle, I'd read while I waited for her. She walked to the bathroom door and turned around and said, "I don't usually do this... One night stands. He seemed nice and he made me feel things I hadn't before."

"Yeah, I understand that. Do you have someone that can come and get you? I'd drive you but I've been drinking. Unless you want to wait until the morning?"

"No, it's ok, I've already called my brother." She produced her phone out of her bra and showed it to me.

"Ok, go get cleaned up and we can wait in here until he arrives."

"Thank you." I smiled at her as she closed the door.

Chapter 13

Mason

I was looking forward to getting Cammie on the back of my bike. The thought of her being pressed up behind me got me excited, but then everything that came to her did. I was sat waiting on my bike for her, smoking a cigarette. I had been waiting for this day to come for a little while now and I was both nervous and excited. What if they didn't like each other? Would I have to choose between them?

"How do I look?" Cammie asked as she strolled towards me, her arms out to her side. She stopped in front of me and twirled round in a circle. She was in dark jeans and a tight hoody, covered by her leather jacket.

"Perfect." Her head dropped and she began kicking around the gravel on the floor with her boot. She sometimes still struggled with her self-confidence, no matter how many times I told her how pretty she was, she never believed me. I pushed her chin up with my finger until I could see her pretty bright blue eyes, I was happy to see no darkness in them. "You ready to go?" She smiled, nodded and climbed onto the bike behind me. I passed her the helmet I bought especially for her, it was black and silver like mine but hers had a couple swirls of purple on it too, her favourite colour.

Once she stopped moving around, I knew she was ready. She had her thighs resting against mine and her arms were clutched tightly around my stomach, she wasn't close enough for my liking. I grabbed her thighs and pulled her so I could feel every inch of her behind me. Once I was satisfied, I took off down the road. Titch held the gates open for us and he nodded his head to us as we rode away.

I loved to get on my bike and just ride, it didn't matter if I had nowhere in particular to go. I loved the feeling of being free, it helped me think and having Cammie close to me, being able to feel her heart beating against my back, made me feel content.

After thirty minutes, I pulled into a housing estate and stopped at the third house on the left, pulling into the gravel driveway and turning off the engine. Cammie climbed off, pulling off her helmet whilst looking around.

"Where are we?" she asked, shaking out her hair. She knew there was no point in tying it up when I was around as I always pulled it down. I loved to see it floating around her shoulders and I could never stop myself from dragging my hands through it when we were close.

"There's someone I want you to meet." I was all of a sudden feeling nervous, I pulled out a cigarette and as I was about to light it, I heard the front door open. I threw the cigarette to the ground and stomped on it even though I never lit it. Just habit I guess.

"I saw that Mason."

"Hi, mum." I smiled at her as she placed her hands on her hips. Cammie's head spun around and looked at my mum. "We'll be up in a second."

"You brought me here to meet your mum? And you didn't even warn me?" Cammie was worrying her bottom lip between her teeth, running her hands through her hair and straightening out her clothes.

"I didn't want you panicking, like you are now." I reached out and grabbed her hand, bringing it up to my lips and kissing her palm.

"Panicking? I'm not panicking?" I wasn't sure who she was trying to convince, herself or me.

"She's going to love you." Cammie took a deep breath. "You ready?" She shook her head and then nodded. I let out a loud laugh and she joined in with me. There was nothing prettier than Cammie when she was smiling.

We linked hands and walked up the couple of steps that led up to the red front door, I pushed it open and we walked in. I could see Cammie taking in everything. Mum wasn't in the living room so we headed towards the kitchen.

"Mum?" I called out.

"In here, honey." She was in the kitchen stirring a large pan that was on the hob.

"Mum." She looked over her shoulder and I pulled Cammie into my side and wrapped my arm around her back. "I want you to meet Cammie, my girlfriend." She wiped her hands on a tea towel as she walked around the large breakfast bar.

"Girlfriend? Why am I only now just hearing about this?"

"It's been busy at the club." I hated having to explain myself to her, she always made me feel like I was twelve and not twenty eight.

"It's nice to meet you, Mrs. Cole," Cammie said, holding her hand out to shake Mum's hand, she grasped her hand in greeting.

"It's nice to meet you too, honey. Would you like a drink? Tea? Coffee? Please, take a seat." Mum waved towards the small kitchen table that was by the patio doors.

"Tea would be great, thanks. Milk with one sugar please." Cammie turned around and went to sit at the table and I heard mum gasp.

"Mum," I said in a warning tone.

"Don't mum me. She's wearing your property jacket, that's more than a girlfriend, Mason. Why did you keep her away from me?" she whisper shouted at me, looking upset, standing there in her red apron. Her dark brown hair was tied up in some sort of twist and her blue eyes looked like they were getting watery. "You never come and visit much anymore, not since…"

"I know, I'm sorry. I'll try better." I pulled her towards me and wrapped my arms around her, she was shorter than me and her head came to my shoulders. "She means a lot to me. I love her, mum. Please make her feel like a part of the family," I whispered into her ear so Cammie couldn't hear. She nodded, wiped the tears from her eyes and turned away to make the drinks.

When I turned around, I saw that Cammie was watching us. She had a confused look on her face and I shook my head for her not to ask. I'd explain it all to her later.

"So, Cammie. Tell me about yourself," mum said as she placed the hot drinks onto the table.

"Um…" She looked at me, worriedly, not sure what to say. "I'm twenty, an only child. I grew up in Devon, I love to read, dance and drink. Mason and my friends are the most important people in my life and one day I'd like to have a dog." She smiled happily at the answer she gave.

"What about your parents? Are they still in Devon?" Cammie quickly grabbed her drink and took a sip, avoiding the question, she never liked to talk about them.

"Nanny?" I looked over towards the door and kept quiet. "Uncle Mason!" She squealed and threw herself at me, luckily I caught her.

"Hey, pumpkin. How are you?" She sat on my lap facing me, legs dangling over mine.

"Good, I had a nap. I went to school this morning, it made me sleepy. Do you know that I have this many friends." She held out her hand holding up four fingers. I laughed at her and she crossed her arms over her chest, frowning at me. "Why are you laughing at me, Uncle Mason? It's not a nice thing to do, is it nanny?"

"No, it's not. You hungry, Emily?" She nodded her head and then her gaze landed on Cammie. Mum got up from the table to make Emily a snack and Cammie was looking at me and Emily.

"Who's the pretty lady?" Emily attempted to whisper in my ear, but she forgot the whole making your voice quiet so she just talked really close to my ear, standing on my lap.

"Emily, I'd like you to meet my girlfriend, Cammie. Cammie this is my niece, Emily."

"Hi, Emily. How old are you?" Cammie asked her. She went shy and hid her face in my neck.

"Cammie asked you a question, young lady," mum said as she pulled items out of the fridge. Emily still didn't speak and she was still hiding.

"You're not shy." I laughed as I tickled her tummy. She giggled, trying to push my hand away. I tickled her again and again until she moved her head away from my neck.

"No, stop. Uncle Mason, no." She laughed as she tried pushing my hand away with her hands and her feet. She was wriggling so much that I placed her on the floor and continued with the torture.

"Are you going to answer Cammie?"

"Yes." She nodded quickly, her blue eyes watering from her laughter. I rose an eyebrow at her and she looked over to Cammie. "I'm four." She smiled.

"That's a good age to be," Cammie told her as I pulled her off the floor and sat her in the spare seat at the table. Mum placed a plate in front of her with a cheese toasty on it.

"Mmm, that looks good," I said, smiling at mum.

"I'll make you one, honey. Cammie would you like one?"

"Yes, she'll have one too. Thanks, mum." I answered for Cammie as I knew she would have said no, she wouldn't want mum going to any trouble for her.

"Why is four a good age to be?" Emily asked Cammie, tipping her to the side. Her brown haired bob moving as she looked between Cammie and her food.

"Well, you get to go to school and play with your friends but you don't have to learn anything difficult. Isn't it fun?"

"Yes, I had to read today. That wasn't as fun as playing."

"I love to read," Cammie announced.

"Really?" Emily scrunched up her face, not understanding why.

"Yes, you can learn new things and get lost in the words, find yourself in a whole new place."

"Like a magic book?" Her eyes lit up and she seemed excited.

"Emily, I think what Cammie means is that you can pretend to be the person in the book going on all the adventures," mum explained as she placed plates in front of Cammie and me.

"Oh!" Emily answered, I wasn't sure if she really understood.

"Thank you," Cammie said.

"Thanks, mum."

"I'm just going to put the washing out to dry," she said as she squeezed my shoulder.

"I'll help!" Emily called out, running after her.

"She's so adorable, why didn't you tell me you have a sister or brother?"

"Had."

"What?"

"I had a sister, she was in an accident. Emily survived and she didn't."

"I'm sorry to hear that." She reached across the table and placed her hand on top of mine. "Where's your dad?"

"He was in the accident too. We lost them both."

"Oh, babe." She got up from her seat and planted herself in

my lap, wrapping her arms over my shoulders and nuzzling into my neck. "I'm sorry."

"I'm ok," I assured her, rubbing my hands up and down her back. We both looked up when the patio door opened and Emily skipped in.

"Is Uncle Mason tickling you too? I'll save you." She ran towards us and took hold of Cammie's hand pulling her away from me.

"Phew, thank you. I didn't think I'd ever get away," Cammie said over dramatically causing Emily to giggle.

"Wanna see my room?" she asked, hopefully.

"I'd love to," Cammie replied and then Emily was dragging her out of the room and up the stairs.

I felt tense and on edge after bringing up my dad and Katie. I hated talking about it but knew that Cammie would have some questions later. I walked outside and sat on the garden bench that was on the patio area, I didn't know where mum had disappeared too but I needed to take the edge off with a cigarette. I couldn't stop the memories that flooded into my head.

"Mason!" I heard mum scream from downstairs. She sounded upset and frantic, I was here visiting for the day, taking a break away from the club. I had been a patched in member for five years and shit was going down. I had come to talk to my dad. He was a patched in member too but had taken a step back recently when he had his last heart attack scare.

As I ran down the stairs, mum was standing by the front door with the phone clutched to her chest and her car keys in her hand. Her eyes were red and she was crying.

"What's wrong? What's happened?"

"There's been an accident, we need to get to the hospital. Quick."

She threw the front door open and ran to the car, her hands were shaking as she tried pressing the central lock button to unlock it.

"I think I should drive." I took the keys off her and opened the passenger door for her. "What's happened?" I asked again as I focused on the road. It was late on Sunday afternoon, it had been raining all day. The roads were stupidly wet and flooded in places but, luckily, the roads were quiet.

"Dad and Katie have been in a car accident. I don't know any more than that," she quietly told me.

"How bad is it? Are they alive?"

"I don't know, Mason!" she snapped. "I'm sorry, I'm just worried."

"It's ok." I placed my hand on hers and held it tightly.

Several minutes later, we pulled into the hospital and I found a parking spot not too far from the entrance. We both climbed out of the car and hurried into the reception. Mum was sobbing as I held her close to me.

"Hi, we're looking for Rob and Katie Cole. We got a call that they were in an accident?"

"And you are?"

"We're family. It's my dad and sister."

"Mr. Cole?" I looked to my right and a nurse dressed in blue scrubs walked towards us. "Please, come with me." I looked at mum and she fisted her hand in my t-shirt as we followed her down the hall and into a room. Looking around, it looked like a smaller waiting area, chairs were lined against the walls and a coffee machine stood next to the large window.

"If you would like to take a seat, I'll get the doctor to come and see you."

"Please, are they ok?" Mum asked, her voice quiet and uneven.

"I'll get the doctor," was all she said as she walked back out of the door; her face was impassive. I hated not knowing what was going on and she gave nothing away. Mum sat down on one of the seats as I paced the room. It felt like we had been waiting ages for the doctor to walk in that door, when in fact it was only minutes.

"Mrs. Cole?" he said as he walked in. Mum stood up and I was in front of him shaking his hand and introducing myself. "You may want to sit down." Oh, shit. That's not good, we didn't want to hear him say that. I steered mum towards the chairs and we both sat down, my arm was wrapped around her and she fisted her hand into my t-shirt again.

"I'm sorry, I'm afraid I have bad news."

"No," Mum whispered, shaking her head.

"Your husband has suffered from a major heart attack, we were unable to save him." I held on tight to mum as she wailed in my arms. Suffered? Heart attack? Unable to save him? These words kept spinning around and around in my head and I couldn't seem to digest them. Mum was shaking next to me and I knew that I had to push my grief aside and be the son she needed me to be. I could hear the doctor talking but it was like there was a bubble around us, a fog, and I couldn't hear him.

"I'm sorry, can you repeat that?" I asked, looking him in the eyes and making sure I didn't let my grip on my mum ease.

"Katie, she had some complications. We tried everything we could, but she didn't make it. I'm sorry."

"No!" Mum screamed, sobbing loudly and I tried to rock her gently. Her breathing was becoming laboured.

"Mrs. Cole, I need you to breathe. Take deep breaths." The doctor was telling her, she was on the verge of a panic attack. Once her breathing was a bit better, I asked;

"The baby?" My sister was nearly at full term in her pregnancy.

"We done an emergency c section and managed to get the baby out, she's fine."

"She?" Mum asked, lifting her head off my shoulder.

"Yes. Would you like to see her?" Mum nodded frantically, using her hands to wipe away her tears and straightened her clothes. Katie and dad gone? What were we going to do? How was mum going to cope losing them both? That little girl was going to have to grow up never knowing how amazing her mum was. Yeah, we fought when we were younger, like all siblings did, but the past two years we had grown closer together. She gave me advice when I needed it like all *big sisters did and I looked after her. I was fiercely protective over her, especially when she came home one day, bags in tow, and announced that she was pregnant. To this day, we still don't know who the dad is, she wouldn't tell us. She said it was better all-around if he never found out.*

"Mason." Mums voiced snapped me out of my head and I looked at her. "Let's go and meet my grandbaby."

A month later and I hadn't left mums side, she had full custody of Emily and looking after her was what kept mum strong. She focused all her energy and time on her. I could hear her crying at night and in the mornings she got on with her day like her heart hadn't been breaking. She was a strong woman and I respected and loved her.

I snapped out of my memories when I felt a familiar pair of hands rest on my shoulders, then they slipped down onto my chest and she kissed the side of my neck. I grabbed her hand and gently pulled her until she was nestled in my lap, which was where she belonged.

"You ok?" she asked, running her hands through my hair as I placed my lips against her neck, it calmed me down to feel her soft skin against me and her pulse beating. I loved having her near and I didn't ever want to lose her. I've lost enough people in my life already.

"I am now." She sat still, knowing that I needed the touch of her, she was the only person who could calm me down like this. Her hand in my hair felt good and soon, I was relaxed and hard. "I need to get you home."

"Oh? And why's that?" she asked as she wriggled in my lap.

"Uncle Mason, are you tickling her again?" Emily asked as she grabbed hold of Cammie's hands, trying to pull her off my lap. I held on tight to Cammie's waist, not wanting Emily to see my arousal.

"I'm not tickling her, I'm cuddling her."

"Oh, why?" She looked confused.

"Because she's my girlfriend and I love her." Emily covered her mouth with her hand, laughing.

"Nanny!" Emily called out, running away. "Uncle Mason loves Cammie. Is she going to be my auntie? Am I going to get cousins?"

I couldn't help but laugh, she made everything in the world better. She was a spitting image of my sister with her brown hair and blue eyes and I would always protect her.

"We better get back," I told Cammie as I gently tapped her ass, telling her she needed to move. She smiled and kissed me quickly before she stood up.

We walked through the house to find mum and Emily watching a film on the TV.

"We gotta get back," I announced.

"It was lovely to see you, honey," Mum said, climbing to her feet and kissing me on the cheek. "And you too, Cammie." She pulled Cammie in for a hug and she looked startled.

"It was great to meet you, Mrs. Cole."

"Oh, please call me Brenda." Cammie smiled at her. "Emily come and say bye to your uncle and Cammie."

"Bye!" she called out, quickly taking her eyes off the TV and waving. We all said our goodbyes and we were soon zooming down the road, Cammie's legs tight against mine. This was what I needed, her close to me, always.

Chapter 14

Cammie

After we got back from visiting Mason's mum we decided to
sit outside and enjoy the sun, it wasn't hot but it was getting
warmer. Mason climbed up and sat on the table of the picnic
bench, his feet resting on the seat. He dug around in his
pocket until he found his cigarettes.

"Nu-uh," I said as I stood on the seat in front of him,
grabbing the cigarettes out of his hand. "I'm not kissing you if
you're smoking."

"Well, it's a good job I'm not smoking then." He smirked at
me, pulling me closer until I was straddled on his lap. His
mouth landed on mine and I dropped the cigarette pack onto
the table so I could thread his hair through my fingers. He had
one hand possessively on my right hip and the other was
behind my neck anchoring me to him. We broke apart when a
car pulled in, I looked over my shoulder and screamed.
Heather was standing by the car, I jumped off Mason's lap
and ran towards her as she held out her arms to me.

"I missed you," she told me.

"I missed you too. Where's my handsome boy?" I pulled
away from her and pulled the back door of the car open.
"There he is. Hi, handsome," I cooed at him. He looked at me,
a big smile on his face and his arms and legs flailed about. I
pulled him out of his car seat and held him close to me. He
was very special to me, especially as I delivered him. I wasn't
sure how I was going to feel once Heather had her baby, I
didn't want to be jealous of her and I wasn't. She had a son
she loved dearly and she also took on Blades two nieces as

well. She was born to be a mother and maybe that just wasn't on the cards for me. Maybe I would have been a terrible mum and if I turned out like mine that would not have been good. I pushed all thoughts aside as Heather asked;

"Where's Daisy?" I looked up from Liam, who was now sitting on my hip and I was making him laugh by tickling him, his laugh was infectious and soon Heather, Blade and Mason were joining in.

"She's in her room. She didn't get home until a couple of hours ago." Heather looked upset and annoyed. Daisy had been on a downward spiral since her husband was killed a few months ago, not that I could blame her. Losing the person you love most in the world would definitely shatter it.

"You go, sugar. I'll get the girls out," Blade said to her, she nodded, kissed him quickly and disappeared into the clubhouse.

"It's good to see you." I smiled at Blade before his arms surrounded me and Liam.

"It's good to see you too, you look happy."

"I am." I smiled looking away from him and focusing on Mason.

Blade moved around the car and got Tegan out, she was still fast asleep in the car seat.

"Hey, VP. Give us a hand will ya?" Blade called out, handing Tegan to him. I reached in the car and pulled out the changing bag and headed into the clubhouse. Liam was gurgling as he was chewing on his fist, drool everywhere. I was covered in it, but his smile made up for it. I sat down next to Carla and watched Kelsey running in and up to Olivia and Danny. They were two of Carla and Prez kids. Mason placed Tegan's car seat on the floor by our feet and she let out a small wail, screwing up her face. Blade bent down to pull her out of her seat and she laid her head on his shoulder and began sucking her thumb.

"Hey, it's good to see you, man," Solar said shaking hands with Blade.

"Is it just me, or does he look hot with a child on his shoulder?" Carla whispered into my ear.

"Oh, it's definitely not you," I agreed with her and we burst out laughing.

"What are you two whispering about?" Mason asked. Liam started wiggling so I stood him up on my lap, looking at him.

"Uncle Mason is so nosey, isn't he Liam?" I cooed in my baby voice. His hand dropped from his mouth, he laughed as he palm connected with my cheek, holding it there. "Nice." I laughed, wiping my face in the shoulder of my jacket.

"Hey!" Ashlyn called out as she walked in the room.

"Ashlyn!" Kelsey called out and ran towards her. Ashlyn had looked after the girls for a few weeks after their mum died so Kelsey was always pleased to see her.

"Hi, sweetie. How are you?" Ashlyn asked as she crouched down onto the floor in front of her.

"Good. We came to see auntie Daisy. You wanna see my colouring?"

"I sure do." As Ashlyn walked over to where the kids were busy colouring and drawing, we heard someone clear their throat and I was surprised to see Cory standing in the entrance to the bar. Ashlyn looked over her shoulder and smiled. "I'll be right back, sweetie." Kelsey nodded, carrying on with what she was doing and when Ashlyn stood up, she looked at me and I rose my eyebrows, telling her we needed to talk about him. I didn't know she was seeing him. I watched her walk towards him and he gave her a smile and looked at her like she was the only person in the room. That was what she needed, a man who would treat her properly. A movement caught my eye and I looked to the right to see

Drake standing behind the bar watching them, he had a scowl on his face. I was convinced that he had a soft spot for her. Cory and Ashlyn walked out of the club hand in hand and I looked over towards the bedrooms when I heard Daisy shout, "No, I don't need you!" She pushed Heather out of the way. "I don't need anyone." She stormed towards the door and almost knocked Ashlyn off her feet.

"Sugar? You ok?" Blade asked as Heather headed towards the door.

"Yeah, I need to follow her. I need to talk to her some more." She was looking from the door to Blade and back again. I stood up and gave him a little nudge telling him to go.

"Let's take the bike," he announced as he walked towards her and passed Tegan to Ashlyn. Heather looked over his shoulder towards me. "Cammie and Ashlyn have got them." I knew she was thinking about the kids, they were her first priority, but Daisy was getting out of control. They left soon after in the hopes of finding her and sorting all of this out.

***

"Hi, are you ok?" I asked as Heather walked into her room looking deflated. I was there as Liam and Tegan were taking a nap and Kelsey and I were watching a DVD on my laptop. The guys were in a church meeting.

"Yeah, I guess." She sighed, walking over and checking on the babies.

"No luck with her?" Heather shook her head and laid out on Kelsey's bed, her feet were dangling off the end.

"Where's Daddy?" Kelsey asked.

"He's working," Heather told her.

"No he's not," she said.

"Yes he is, little monster." Heather jumped off the bed and grabbed Kelsey, throwing her in the air and then tickling her.

She let out a little scream of laughter. "Time to get you ready for bed."

"Can I have a bath?"

"Yes, ok." She turned back to me. "Thanks for looking after them today."

"You don't need to thank me, I love doing it." I stood up from the bed and pulled her in for a hug. "You can only try your best with her. Love you."

"Love you too. See you in the morning."

"Oh, I'm starting my new job tomorrow but I'll be back by early afternoon."

"You can tell me all about it tomorrow." She smiled and I left her in peace to get Kelsey ready for bed.

Chapter 15

Mason

"We'll check it out tomorrow night," Prez said. "Now get out of here." He slammed the gavel down and the room emptied pretty quickly. I was heading for the door. "VP?"

"Yeah?"

"You gonna be able to keep your cool tomorrow? No barging in there? We do this my way."

"You're the Prez."

"Just remember that." I nodded and headed for the door. Toes had finally got Intel on the two guys that we were looking for. I couldn't wait to get my hands on the guy who took Cammie away from her home and the one who tortured her. My hands balled into fists and I felt the adrenaline run through my body. They will get what's coming to them. I looked around the bar area for Cammie and there was no sign of her, I felt like I was a right pussy always looking for her but my body was drawn to hers and I was completely addicted to her, that was one habit that I didn't want to break. I headed back to our room and the sight before me made me smile. Cammie was laying on our bed, she was in tiny bed shorts and a strappy top, no bra. Her toes were wiggling on the bed, her pink toe nails caught my eye. She was reading and her eyes didn't leave her kindle even after I walked into the room. I stood still and watched her for a few seconds. Was she reading a raunchy book? Her toes wiggled when she was being teased and also when she was close to her release. Her left leg came up and rubbed against her right one, I was right, she was reading a naughty book and it was turning her on.

"You gonna just stand there all night? Or you gonna join me over here?" she asked not looking away from her book. I threw my leather cut onto the sofa and kicked off my boots and socks before I climbed onto the bed. She placed her kindle onto the bedside table and pulled her hair out of the bun that was on top of her head, I laughed to myself as she was saving me a job. It would have been the first thing that I would have done.

"Aren't you going to show me what you were reading?" She shook her head, her tongue darted out of her mouth to wet her lips. My eyes took all of her in and her nipples were starting to harden underneath the thin material. I straddled her hips and brushed her nipple with the back of my hand and she immediately arched into me. I couldn't stop the smile from forming on my face, I loved how responsive she was to my touch. I sat back on my heels and looked at her. She was smiling and her blue eyes were even brighter than usual. I took hold of her hand and sat her up so I could undress her, she obliged and was rewarded when I sucked her nipple into my mouth.

"Mason," she gasped as she held my head closer. I laughed and the vibrations must have coursed through her body as she tried to move underneath me. "Please," she pleaded, releasing her hold on me to attack the button on my jeans. Once she had my jeans undone, she slipped her hand inside and that was my undoing, I pushed at her shoulder gently and she fell back onto the bed, her breasts bouncing. I pulled at her shorts until she was underneath me completely naked, this was how I liked her and I loved that she no longer shied away from me. I jumped off the bed and quickly undressed, not letting my eyes leave hers. She wiggled on the bed, showing me that she was ready for me. I approached the side of the bed and pulled at her hips until they were hanging off the edge slightly. I dropped to my knees pulling her legs over my shoulders and I started raining kisses all over her body, ending at her clit where my mouth just hovered above it. I knew what she wanted and I wanted her to be so turned on that one swipe would have her coming for me. I ran my stubble up and down the inside of her thighs, grabbing hold of her ass and squeezing it. I angled her body towards my mouth more, she was mainly resting on her shoulders, that's why I didn't want this to take long. I ran my tongue from her entrance to her clit and gently nibbled. She moaned and held her breath, one swipe, two swipes, and on the third one, she released her breath and cried out in pleasure. I was painfully hard, but needed her ready for me. I grabbed at the condom that I threw on the bed and covered myself. We really needed to get her on the pill so I didn't have to bother with these things. As I stood up, she wound her legs around my hips and I placed my arm under her back holding on to the back of her neck so I could reposition her on the bed. I didn't let go of the hold I had on her, I used my other hand to unhook her legs and position myself at her entrance. She tried to move her hips so that I would slip into her but my body on top of hers was restricting her movements.

"Please, Mason," she panted. "I need you in me."
I wasn't going to deny her what she wanted, I pushed inside in one long thrust, her warmth enveloping me; her wetness made it easy to move. With the hold I had on the back of her neck, I pulled her body down and I drove deeper into her, capturing her mouth in a tantalising kiss. She pulled her legs up to my sides.

"Harder, please, harder!" she called out. I unhooked my arm from under her and pulled her legs up so the back of her thighs were resting against my body. As I bent forward to start moving again, I was pushing her legs closer to her chest.

"You don't need harder, you need deeper," I panted, not letting up on my fast pace.

"Yes, yes," she agreed with me. I could feel the sweat forming on my forehead, I pushed my hands down on her legs and increased my speed once more, I just had to hold off a little bit more, I wanted to feel her coming around me first. Seconds later, she was calling out my name, her body was squeezing me and I shot off, the pleasure riding up my back and my body hummed.

"Fuck, that was hot." I smiled as I released the hold I had on her legs and she dropped them to the bed. She hadn't said anything, her chest was rising and falling at a rapid pace. "You ok?"

"Hmmm mmmm." I laughed at her tired voice and I pulled out of her and ripped the condom off, tying a knot in the end and throwing it in the bin. I placed my arm back under her back and raised her off the bed, pulling the duvet down and settling her on the cool sheets. She sighed in pleasure as her eyes fluttered closed. I climbed in beside her and pulled her into my body.

"I love you."

"Love you," she mumbled, sleepily.

Chapter 16

Cammie

I groaned as I woke up and stretched, I hadn't slept that well in I don't know how long.

"You ok?" Mason whispered from behind me into my ear.

"Mmm hmm. Just aching, but in a good way." I smiled as I rolled over to face him. I placed my hand on his stubbled jaw and looked into his pale blue eyes, those were eyes I could get lost in forever. Forever? I liked the sound of that and for the first time in a long time that didn't scare me.

"Will you tell me what happened to your dad and sister?" Mason groaned as he turned away from me slightly and laid on his back. He raised the arm closest to me in the air and looked at me, nodding his head to tell me to curl up with him. I placed my head on his tattooed chest and traced the lines of the tribal dragon that covered it.

"I had been patched into the crusaders for about six years, I lived here. This was my life, my dad was a member too but he suffered from a heart attack scare and mum made him cut back. No long rides, no stress and no living at the clubhouse. I mean, they had their home too but once we were older, sometimes they would stay here, it was just easier." I nodded, I completely understood that, a lot of bikers had their own homes as well as the clubhouse. I wonder why Mason didn't?

"Anyway, dad was always on at me as I didn't visit very often and once my sister came home pregnant refusing to tell us who the baby's dad was, I started spending more time with them. Katie went off and moved to London a few years earlier."

"Was she older than you?"

"Yeah but only by two years. I was spending a day at home with the family on a wet Sunday, we were watching movies and playing board games, you know all the cheesy family stuff." No, I didn't know. My parents had never spent that sort of time with me, I was always told to entertain myself.

"Katie wanted some ice cream, a particular flavour as she was craving it. Dad didn't want her driving in the rain so he took her."

He told me everything that had happened with them, how Emily was born and how his mum had full custody of her as they didn't know who her dad was. He was emotional and I was happy that he had shared that part of his life with me. I loved that behind closed doors he was exactly who I needed, a strong, passionate man who loved his family. His no nonsense attitude when he was in VP mode was hot as hell to watch too. I raised his arm in the air so I could look at what time it was on his watch.

"I've gotta get up," I grumbled, rolling away from him. "Today is my first day at work and Dan said about some paperwork that I needed to fill in so I'm gonna head in early." I swung my legs over the side of the bed and raised my arms above my head, stretching out my sore muscles again. I yelped when Mason grabbed my hips and pulled me back against him.

"You're teasing me," he whispered in my ear.

"I'm not, I'm just stretching." I smiled at the thought that I could wind him up so easily. I knew that I had a decent figure, big breasts, slim hips and a flat stomach with a horrible scar that was slowly fading with the cream that Mason gave me to use. But nothing made me smile more than knowing that Mason couldn't keep his hands off me.

I wiggled my way out of his grasp and headed into the

bathroom, I didn't want to be late on my first day of work. I was excited to be doing something different, maybe this way, once I was earning a decent wage, we could look into getting our own house. I liked staying at the clubhouse, it was familiar, I felt safe and protected even when Mason wasn't there but I didn't want us being there in the long term.

I was rinsing the shampoo out of my hair as the bathroom door opened, I looked through the steamed glass to find Mason leaning against the bathroom sink, one foot crossed over the other and his hands gripping onto the sink behind him.

"Why don't you have your own house?"

"Never needed one, babe." His eyes were watching every part of my body as I got myself ready for the day. I turned off the shower, opened the glass door and grabbed the towel that was laying on the closed toilet seat.

"Do you like living here? At the clubhouse?" I bent over, wrapped in my towel to towel dry my hair, I didn't want it dripping down my back. When I looked up at him he was staring at my ass and not answering the question. "Mason?" His eyes shot to mine and he winked at me.

"Yeah, I like living here. Don't you?" He scratched his stubble on his face with his hand as he turned around towards the sink to fill it up with water.

"Yeah, I do. I'd just like for us to have our own place too. Once I'm earning good money, then we can afford it."

"I can afford it, babe." He splashed water onto his face and covered it in shaving foam.

"What do you mean you can afford it? Wait, why are you shaving?" I grasped his arm to stop him taking the first glide with his razor.

"It's itching. I've lived here for the last ten years, earnt money and never spent it, except for my bike." I watched as he ran the razor down his cheek, I was trying to remember if I had ever seen him stubble free. He laughed at me watching him. "Aren't you going to be late?"

"Shit, yeah." I hurried through the open bathroom door and got ready for my day. I decided on a simple pair of jean shorts and a t-shirt. I couldn't be bothered to blow dry my hair, I plaited it so it fell over my left shoulder.

"I'll walk you down," Mason said as he engulfed me in his arms from behind and rubbed his smooth face against mine. I actually liked it, it was soft.

"Don't be silly. I'll be fine. See you in a few hours." I squeezed his forearms that were wrapped around my middle and he loosened his grip so I could face him. "Love you." I stretched up on my tiptoes and planted a kiss on his lips.

"Love you too, call me if you need me." I nodded, kissed him again and headed out of the clubhouse and down the beach.

***

Mason

I was glad that I had opened up to Cammie and told her about my family, I never wanted there to be secrets between us, well except for the club business ones. I wouldn't put her in danger by telling her anything.

After I had my morning smoke, I needed coffee. I was in the kitchen waiting for the kettle to boil when the kitchen door opened. I looked over my shoulder and was surprised to see Cammie walking in.

"Hey, you ok? Why aren't you at work? What did they do to you? Do I need to kick some ass?" I had my hands gripped firmly onto Cammie's hips and looked at her directly in the eye. She was smiling and laughing at me.

"Calm down, unless you want a fight with the freezer?" I was confused, what was she going on about. "Babe, the freezer at the shop has packed in, all the stock has melted. Dan told me to start next week instead. You making coffee?"

"Yeah, you want one?" She nodded. "Go and sit down and I'll bring it over." She proceeded to sit at the breakfast bar as I poured the hot water into the two mugs.

"Morning," Blade grumbled as he lumbered into the kitchen clutching hold of two baby bottles.

"Hi, how's Heather?" Cammie asked him. I picked up the two mugs and placed one in front of her, she smiled at me and then focused back on Blade, waiting to hear his answer.

"Not great, we're heading home today. Daisy doesn't want to be helped and it's upsetting Heather being here." He filled the kettle up with water and flicked the switch to boil it.

"Oh, I was hoping you were going to stay longer. I miss you all." She pouted.

"Yeah, about that… How do you fancy coming back for a few days? Ashlyn too?" He leant against the kitchen side looking at her.

"Oh, I would love that." She clasped her hands together excitedly. "Babe, you don't mind do you?" She looked over to me, her eyes were lit up and although I didn't want her to go, didn't want to be apart from her, how could I say no?

"I'm not overly happy about it," I complained, taking a sip of my coffee. She jumped off her stool and rounded the breakfast bar to stand in front of me.

"It'll only be for a few days, Heather needs me."

"Fine, but Drake goes with you." I needed to know she was safe, Devon was the place those scumbags took her and although we knew they were in Cornwall it didn't put my mind at ease, what if they were watching her or Ashlyn? Wanted them back?

"We don't need a prospect with us, we'll have Blade." She

dismissed what I had demanded. I could feel the agitation on my skin.

"Cammie," I warned her.

"Fine, ok… I'm going to tell Ashlyn, then I need to pack." She pecked me on the lips and rushed towards the kitchen door.

"Let's surprise Heather later?" Blade said before she left the room, she nodded and strolled away.

"Thanks, man," I said to Blade who now had the milk for the babies ready.

"What?" He chuckled, he knew exactly how I was feeling.

"I have to be separated from my girl now, not happy." I walked over to the sink, rinsed my cup out and placed it in the dishwasher. The Prez's Old Lady was always on at us to clean up after ourselves, that's what the club bunnies were for, right?

"I'm sure you're dick can cope for a couple of days." He laughed as he ambled towards the kitchen door, the bottles in one hand and a cup of coffee in the other.

"Don't think it can, man."

"You've always got a hand." He winked as he left the room, laughing. I bet he thought it was a big laugh taking my Old Lady away from me, it wasn't just about sex for me, it was knowing that she was safe.

Chapter 17

Mason

"VP, do not go in all guns blazing. We don't want to have to bring you out in a body bag. Keep a cool head about it," Prez said to me as the six of us were crouched down talking behind our large van. We were at the Satans new clubhouse in Cornwall, I was out for blood and there were only two people on my radar; Preppy and Switch. "We get what we came here for, Preppy and Switch. No one messes with our girls, I won't have Cammie and Ashlyn in fear, them constantly looking over their shoulders. They need peace and we're going to give it to them."

"We can kill everyone else though?" Toes asked.

"Let's end this club once and for all," Prez announced. "Titch, you stay here with the van. Get it ready for when we bring Preppy and Switch out."

"Got it, Prez."

"Everyone has seen the Intel, we know who we're looking for. Let's go and get them, boys."

We had hashed out the plan in church today, Solar and Toes were taking the back entrance, Tat was going to get anyone outside that tried to escape with the back up from Titch and me and Prez were going in through the front door.

We stayed low as we dodged around the cars, bins and anything that would keep us hidden. There was no one outside and only a few lights were on inside. As far as we knew, the Satans were no longer a big club after Blade and his club stormed their clubhouse and killed everyone in sight.

"Shit!" Prez swore as we heard gun shots. We took off

running towards the front of the abandoned warehouse. I kicked the door open and Prez entered first, shooting as soon as he was inside. I followed him in, two dead bikers were laying in the open plan room and there wasn't a lot of furniture which made it easier to see if anyone was trying to hide. I kept my gun up and aimed in front of me at all times, ready to shoot. We heard a commotion at the other end of the house and marched our way towards it.

We stopped dead in our tracks when we were face to face with Preppy and Switch, they both had a gun each to Solar and Toes's head.

"Looky what we got here," Preppy laughed. "We've caught ourselves some Cornish Crusaders." Prez and I both had our guns pointed at them.

"Drop them," Switch demanded. When we didn't lower our guns he shouted, "Or does your club want to be down four members, a VP and a Prez as well?"

I saw out of the corner of my eye that Prez was lowering his gun and although I didn't want to, I had to do the same as well. We were not going to lose two brothers, not here, not tonight.

"What do you want?" Preppy asked. "What are you doing here?" We all stayed quiet and I saw movement out of the corner of my eye, I didn't want to alert them to it so I stayed still. I was sure it was Tat, looking in through the window. What was he planning?

"Answer me!" Preppy yelled, pushing the nose of his gun further into Toes head. We stayed quiet and I noticed his eyes were flitting around the room, shit, I didn't want for him to notice Tat so I unleashed my hate towards the pair of them.

"You, we want you both dead," I snarled. "You took what didn't belong to you…"

"That's what we do." Preppy laughed, cutting me off. My

blood boiled, rage surged through my body and I lunged towards them, hoping like hell that they wouldn't pull the trigger. A loud crash echoed around us and a van, our van, with Titch behind the wheel crashed through the side of the building startling us all. Debris flew everywhere knocking us all off our feet. I scrambled to find my gun, these guys were not getting away from us. Solar had Switch pinned to the floor, pounding into his face over and over again and I caught a glimpse of something dark in the corner of my eye, I whipped my head around to see Preppy trying to flee. I aimed my gun and shot at his shoulder, he stumbled and fell to the ground. He attempted to get up and as he did, Tat appeared in front of him and kicked him in the face, knocking him out.

***

We had managed to get both Switch and Preppy tied up and in the back of the van, Titch drove them back to the clubhouse as we all followed. They were not getting away from us now. Once we had all pulled into the compound, Titch drove straight to the back entrance of the building and we all parked our bikes along the fence by the clubhouse doors. As I climbed off, my phone started vibrating in my pocket. Shit, I didn't have time for that now. I ignored it and strolled towards where Titch, Toes and Solar were getting Preppy and Switch out of the back of the van.

"You ok to handle this, VP?" Prez asked me, halting me in my steps.

"Yeah, I got it. You go be with your family."

"Want me to call the doc? For his shoulder?"

"Na, we'll let him bleed out for a bit." I chuckled as Prez slapped me on the shoulder and headed into the clubhouse. Once I got into the back entrance of the clubhouse and down the stairs to the small room under the house, the guys had

Preppy and Switch tied up, they were both sitting on the floor tied to large concrete pillars. Solar had done a good job on Switch's face, he had a cut above his eyebrow, both his eyes were swelling shut and he had a bruise across his jaw.

"Now, what are we going to do to you?" I said as I paced in front of them both.

"Getting me fixed up for a start would be great," Preppy said.

"Now, why would we wanna do that, when you'll be dead soon." Solar laughed.

"Well, if we're going to be dead soon there is no use in talking." Preppy laughed. "You won't be getting any info out of us, ain't that right, S..." Toes shut him up by pressing his hand over the bullet wound in Preppy's right shoulder.

"We don't have you here for info, just good old fashioned revenge." I chuckled.

"Just get on with it," Switch grumbled.

"No way, waiting will make it more pleasurable," I whispered in his ear. "Have a good night." I turned on my heel and walked out of the room with Solar, Toes and Tat behind me. "You." I pointed at Titch. "Good job back there, you got us out of a sticky situation. Stay on guard here, don't let anyone in or out."

"Sure thing, VP."

We all went our separate ways whilst I stayed outside to have a smoke. I was glad that I finally had my hands on them, they soon were going to regret messing with my Old Lady. Speaking of Cammie, I had only heard from her once since she had left and that was to let me know they got to Heather and Blade's house ok. I pulled my phone out of my pocket to see I had four missed calls and a text message. I clicked on the notification to see who they were from, all from Cammie. Shit. I opened the text message.

Hope everything is ok. Going to sleep now. Night Mason, I love you x x x x

Shit, it was two in the morning, it was way too late to be calling her back so I replied to the message instead.

Sorry, babe. We were out on a run. Just got back. Call you tomorrow. Love you too x

I walked in the clubhouse in desperate need for a drink, I ambled my way to the bar and sat on the stool.

"Whiskey," I demanded from Penny. She smiled and placed the glass in front of me.

"Tough night?"

"Something like that." I downed the drink and pushed the glass towards her asking for more. She topped it up, leaning over the bar with her tits on full display.

"I can help you relax if you want?" She licked her lips and looking at her made me feel sick to my stomach, why did I ever touch these bunnies? They were nothing compared to Cammie. My Cammie. Fuck, she had only been gone for one day and I missed the fuck out of her already.

"Why would I do anything to jeopardise what I have with Cammie?"

"She never has to know." She placed her hand on top of mine and I pulled away instantly. These girls were too needy and I hated that. I grabbed my full glass and turned around to walk away, maybe a game of pool would help relax me. I went to head in that direction when I saw Cory, the bloke Ashlyn had been seeing and his mate Dan, Cammie's new boss. I made a beeline for them, I needed to have a word with that guy.

"Dan," I growled.

"Oh, hey, Holes."

"Holes." Cory nodded to me. I didn't take my eyes off Dan.

"A word." I jerked my head telling him I needed it in private. I began to walk away and he obediently followed behind me. I lead him outside, I needed another smoke. I looked towards the back of the clubhouse and smiled just knowing what was in the cellar. It took every ounce of willpower not to go down there and shoot the shit out of them. I pulled my cigarettes out of my pocket and lit one, keeping my back to Dan.

"What can I do for you, Holes?" I spun around and crowded him against the wall.

"First off, you treat my girl good. She doesn't need to work but chooses to. If I catch you eye fucking her the way you did when we first walked in, I'll remove those pretty little grey eyes of yours. If I catch you touching her, standing too close to her, breathing the same air as her, I won't be held responsible for my actions. She is mine, only mine. Got that?" He nodded, eyes wide from fear. I took a step back and gave him a look to tell him to get lost. As he was scurrying away, I yelled out, "And wear a t-shirt when you're around her."

I finished my smoke, stomped on the butt and headed back into the clubhouse. A game of pool and poker were needed.

Chapter 18

Mason

"What do you mean you're not coming home for a few more days?" I paced the small area in my bedroom as I spoke with Cammie on the phone. She had already been gone over a week and I was getting frustrated. I needed to see her, hold her in my arms and make sure that she was ok.

"Heather needs our help."

"I need you here with me, you're the VPs Old Lady."

"Mason, don't start..."

"I've had enough, I'm coming to get you myself."

"If your dick ever wants to see action again, you'll stay where you are. It's only a couple more days. I don't wanna fall out over this." I hung my head at the tone of her voice, she sounded quiet. I rubbed my hand over the back of my neck.

"Yeah I know, I just miss you that's all."

"I miss you too." My head shot up when there was a knock on my bedroom door. "Shit, I gotta go. Love you."

"Love you too." I pressed the end button and threw my phone onto the bed.

"Yeah?" I called out. Tat poked his head around my door.

"Don't forget we got those girls coming in today."

"What girls?" I didn't have a clue what he was going on about, did the Prez bring in more bunnies?

"The ones for piercings and tattoos."

"Shit, I completely forgot."

"There's six of them, man. Two want tattoos, three want piercings and one wants a tat and a piercing."

"When are they gonna be here?"

"In ten minutes."

"Let's get set up then." We walked out of the clubhouse and to the small building that held mine and Tat's tattoo and piercing business. We didn't usually work in the evenings but Tat had booked them in. I think that secretly, he was hoping to have fun with one or more of them.

I was sitting at my station, all my equipment was freshly sterilised and I had a display cabinet that held all of the jewellery. The only thing that separated Tat and me was a curtain between us.

The bell above the door of the shop chimed and Tat was on his feet eagerly greeting the girls.

"Hello, Ladies!" he called out and as I walked out through to the reception of the shop all eyes glued to mine.

"Hi, Holes." One of the girls smiled. She was tiny, with long blonde hair, short shorts on and a tight v neck t-shirt. She already had a lip piercing, did I do that? I never remembered my clients.

"Hey. Did I do that one?" I asked, nodding towards her lip.

"See, I told you he'd remember me," she said to the girl who was stood beside her. She sauntered over to me slowly, "Yes, and these. I'm Debbie." She grabbed my hands and placed them on her breasts where through the thin material of her top and no bra, I could feel her nipple piercings. I pulled my hands away and took a step back.

"Let's get this done. Who is having what?"

"I want my lip pierced!" A tall, leggy brunette called out.

"Me too," her shorter friend with spiky black hair added.

"I want a rose tattoo," a curvier girl said, she had brown curly hair.

"I want a star tattoo," another girl with brown, straight hair answered, and I had to take another glance, they were in fact twins.

"And I want my clit pierced and a tattoo. Oh and Nancy couldn't make it tonight, she'll call and make another appointment." The blonde from earlier said as she stepped closer to me again. What was her name again? Debbie?

"Well, let's start with you," Tat said pointing at Debbie. "What do you want and where, sweetheart?"

"I want a row of butterflies on the inside of my thigh." She placed her leg up onto the chair behind the desk and pointed to where she wanted it. She was talking to Tat but eyeballing me.

"Let's have a look at some designs." He led her away.

"Right, girls. Let's do these lip piercings." I held back the curtain that offered privacy form the reception and they walked through. Tat wasn't in his section yet so I didn't close the curtain between us. "Here's the jewellery display, have a look and see what you want. The prices are on there." As they looked at what jewellery they wanted, I got my equipment ready. Just as the first girl got comfy in the chair, her friend Debbie stripped off her shorts in Tat's section. I stood up and went to draw the curtain.

"No, don't. I want to watch." I rose my eyebrow at her in question. "It'll help distract me. We're all friends," she said as she stood in front of me in a v neck t-shirt that was too tight, showing that her nipples were pierced and aroused and a scrap of material that wouldn't be classed as underwear. I'm sure Tat would be getting an eyeful once she spreads her legs for him to tattoo her.

"What's your name sweetheart?" I asked the girl sitting in my chair.

"Carly."

"You nervous?" I sat on my stool and wheeled myself so I was in front of her, my legs spread wide so I could fit her legs in between mine.

"A little."

"Ok, first I'm just going to mark the position with this pen and you can tell me if it's where you want it." She nodded as I drew the small dot on her mouth. I held up the small mirror so she could see, she smiled and nodded once more. "Here we go." I cleaned the area, grabbed the clamp and put it in position but as I was about to pierce it, she grabbed her friends hand and squeezed her eyes shut. A quick pop of the needle going through her skin and I threaded through the piercing and tightened the ball onto the end.

"All done."

"Really? Wow, that was quick." She smiled and winced at the same time. I went through the cleaning instructions with her and her friend at the same time, saved myself time saying it twice.

"You ready?" I asked the girl with the spiky black hair as I removed my latex gloves.

"Yep." I patted the seat and drew on her with the pen so she could tell me if that's where she wanted it. "Looks good."

"Ok, let me sort out the equipment and I'll be right there." I discarded the previous needle and got a fresh one out, disinfected the clamp and pulled on a fresh pair of gloves.

"Here we go," I told her as I went through the same motions as before. This one wasn't as scared as her friend, she didn't flinch, screw up her face or wince. I was impressed.

"My turn next." I looked to my right and Debbie was talking to me. Tat was cleaning her up and covering her tattoo.

"Yeah, I'll just have a quick smoke and then be with you."

"I'll join you," Tat said as he pulled off his latex gloves and we walked outside. Once my cigarette was lit, I pulled out my phone and sent Cammie a quick text.

Can't wait for you to come home, the beds lonely without you x

"You turning into a pussy, man." Tat laughed as he slapped

me on the back, reading over my shoulder.

"That's what happens when you find the right girl." I smiled.

"That Debbie chick sure is hot. I was working on her tat between her legs and she got a wet patch on her panties. She wants me, man."

"You can't fuck her once I've done her piercing."

"No, I can't fuck her pussy. She's got two more holes, dude." He laughed.

"Let's get this shit done and go for a drink." Tat nodded in agreement.

We walked back in and Tat was talking to the next girl wanting a tattoo and Debbie was sitting in the chair waiting for me.

"You sure about this?" I asked her as I sat down onto my stool in front of her.

"Have you fucked someone with a clit piercing before?"

"Yeah," I answered as I pulled on my latex gloves and got the needle and jewellery ready.

"Maybe you can show me how good it feels after?"

"He has an Old Lady but I can show you, sweetheart." Tat winked at her. Her eyes lit up and she raised her legs in the air and pulled her panties off, showing him everything.

I grabbed the picture highlighting the parts of the pussy.

"So you want your clit pierced?" I pointed to the picture.

"Oh, no. That bit." She blushed, pointing to the hood over the clit.

"Right, you want the hood pierced, vertical or horizontal?"

"Um... What do you suggest?" she asked biting on her bottom lip.

"It's not up to me, sweetheart. You have to live with it. VCH is the most popular."

"VCH?" she asked. Shit, do these girls not research what they want to have done? So many people come in wanting one piercing but it's not what they actually want. The guys get confused by an APA piercing and a Prince Albert and the girls get confused between an actual clit piercing and a hood piercing.

"Vertical clitoral hood."

"Oh, yeah I want one of those." She spread her legs wide and I pushed them back together.

"You need your legs only open slightly else the area will be stretched. Lie back down." She got herself comfy and Tat was still watching. "You not got work to do?"

"I wanna watch, you don't mind do you Debbie?" She bit her bottom lip and shook her head.

"I need to test the area to make sure it can be done."

"Ok, how do you do that?" Her voice wavered and I was sure the nerves were catching up with her.

"I'm going to use this cotton swab." I showed it to her as she leant up on her elbows. "And place it under the hood and see if I can see it… Yep, perfect for piercing." I discarded the cotton swab and grabbed the needle. "Ready?"

"Yep."

"Keep very still." I parted her lips and pushed the needle up through her hood in a quick but steady motion. "The needle is through, I've just got to add the jewellery." I got it into position and pulled the needle away as the jewellery slid it. "This is a nice one you chose. A curved one looks good. You can change the jewellery after about four weeks, experiment with different sizes and see what brings you the most pleasure."

"Ah, thank you." She flew off the seat and flung her arms around my neck, kissing me on the cheek. I didn't touch her back except when I tried to push her away. I ran through all of the cleaning instructions and she got dressed.

After my area was cleaned and disinfected, I looked over to

Tat.

"You need me to stay?"

"Na, man. I got it." I nodded, pulled my leather cut back on and dug out a cigarette for when I was outside.

"Thanks, ladies." I smiled. "If you have any problems come back and see me."

"Thanks, Holes." Debbie smiled. I nodded my head in her direction and escaped through the front door. I lit up my cigarette as soon as I was outside and headed for the main club house. My phone vibrated in my pocket and I pulled it out to see Cammie's face lighting up the screen.

"Hi, beautiful," I answered.

"Hey." She whispered.

"You ok, Cam?"

"Yep, just trying to be quiet. Ashlyn is asleep. I missed your voice."

I laughed as I took a drag of my cigarette.

"We only spoke a couple hours ago, have you been drinking?"

"Maybe." I could hear rustling and wondered what she was doing.

"Are you in bed?"

"Yes," she whispered and my dick jumped in my trousers, she said it just like she did when I penetrated her.

"Go downstairs, Cammie."

"I can't. Drake is sleeping on the sofa." She giggled.

"Go into the bathroom, put that hand of yours down your sleep shorts and make yourself wet."

"Mason!" she whisper shouted at me. "I can't. What if Ashlyn hears me?"

"You don't have to say anything, I'll do all the talking." I could hear more rustling and then a click of a door, my girl was being good and listening to me.

"Where are you?"

"Outside the clubhouse." I drew one last lingering drag of my cigarette before stomping it out.

"You can't talk to me out there."

"There's no one around, everyone's inside." I sat down on the picnic bench, closed my eyes and pictured Cammie in my head. "Now, sit down on the toilet seat, lean back and picture me standing above you. My breath is on your neck, making the hairs stand on end and my stubble is scratching down and across your collarbone. The tips of my fingers are dragging over your hardened nipples. Touch them, sweetheart; pull them, tease them." Her breath picked up and I could hear the arousal in her soft moans. "Part your legs, imagine me standing in between them. My hands are gliding over your thighs, the roughness makes you squirm. Trail that hand of yours down and into your sleep shorts. You're wet for me, soaked. Dip a finger inside for me, Cammie." She gasped and my dick throbbed. I palmed it through my jeans, trying to calm it down. "Drag the juices up to your clit and rub a slow circle around it, getting faster each time." Her breath sounded laboured, I knew she was getting close. "Keep rubbing, baby. This is the only way I'll let you come without me, that pussy of yours is for me to penetrate only. I own it, it's mine. That's it, Cam. I can hear that you're close, so close baby. When you come home, the first thing I'm going to do is taste you, run my pierced tongue all over that soft flesh of yours until you come on my face." A little murmur from her lets me know that she was successful, I could picture her now, a flush covering her face and her breasts rising and falling with each breath she's trying to calm. "You ok, Cam?"

"Mmmm hmmmm."

"Get yourself to bed and come home soon. I love you."

"Love you too."

Fuck, that was hot. I missed her. I needed a drink.

Chapter 19

Mason

"VP you ready?" Prez shouted to me as he walked into the bar. I nodded, climbed off my stool and followed him out of the clubhouse and down to the back entrance. It was a sunny morning, not many clouds in the sky and I was itching to get out on my bike for a ride. I just knew that if I climbed on it, the first place I'd be driving would be to Devon and Cammie told me stay away.

Prez got to the bottom steps and Titch was standing outside of the door.

"How are they?"

"Preppy has lost a lot of blood, he is in and out of consciousness."

"And Switch?" I asked.

"Still as cocky as ever."

We walked past Titch and into the dark, smelly cellar. Preppy was sitting there with his head drooping to the side and Switch smiled as we walked in.

"What the fuck are you smiling about?" I asked.

"Just remembering how sweet her cunt was, how fuckable. Shame I never got to fuck her tonsils. There's always time yet."

I pulled my gun out and aimed it at his head. "Shut the fuck up!" I yelled.

"VP, he's doing this on purpose. Trying to get an easy way out."

"I don't want to be dead!" he yelled. "My brothers will come, they'll know it was you that took us. They'll be here."

"Let them come, then we can kill each and every one of you fuckers. You give all us bikers a bad name," Prez sneered at him. "In the meantime, we'll let Titch have a little play with you guys. Titch…"

"Prez."

"Feel free to practice your torture methods on these guys." His smile grew on his face and he wiped his hands on his jeans and pulled a set of knives out of his back pocket.

"My pleasure."

We walked away to the sound of screams and excited laughter.

***

Cammie

"What time did Blade say they would be back?" I asked Drake as I sat down onto the sofa after getting the kids in bed. They had been gone hours and I was expecting them home by now.

"Not sure, I'll give him a call." Drake walked away as Ashlyn came into the room.

"I'm all packed, you excited to be getting home?"

"Yeah, I miss Mason. Though I'm gonna miss all of them. How about you? Missing Cory?"

"No, we're just having a bit of fun. Nothing more than that." She waved her hand in the air dismissing the conversation as she sat down in the recliner and pulled her feet under her.

"There's no answer, it's turned off," Drake said as he came back in.

"That's strange…" I was cut off by the house phone, I leant forward and grabbed the black cordless phone off the coffee table.

"Hello?" I answered.

"Oh god, Cammie." Heather sobbed.

"Heather?"

"Hey, Cammie. How's the kids?" Blade asked as I heard Heather sobbing in the background.

"They're all good. Just put them to bed. What time are you coming back? Is Heather ok?"

"There's been a bit of a problem, I need to talk to Drake." I looked around and saw that Ashlyn was listening intently and Drake had disappeared.

"Yeah ok. Drake!" I called out. He rushed around the corner. "It's Blade." I handed him the phone and he walked away. I looked at Ashlyn and shrugged my shoulders. We patiently waited for Drake to come back and once he rounded the corner he was no longer on the phone.

"What's going on?"

"All I can tell you is that we need to get the kids up, pack an overnight bag for them and get back to the Cornish Crusaders." I opened my mouth to speak and Drake cut me off. "Please, Cam, don't make this more difficult for me."

"Ok, I'll get Liam and Tegan." I turned to Ashlyn. "Can you get Kelsey up?" She nodded and we hurried upstairs.

Once the car was packed with bags and the kids were strapped in, we were off heading back home. I was excited to see Mason but I felt apprehensive about why we needed to go back and where Heather and Blade were.

***

Mason

I had just put out my smoke and was about to head back into the clubhouse when I heard the metal gates scrape open and the sound of a car and a bike. I waited to see who it was and was glad to see Ashlyn's car pull in. As soon as it stopped, I yanked open the passenger door and pulled Cammie out.

"I missed you," I told her. "What are you all doing here? Where's Heather and Blade?"

"VP?" I looked up to see Drake nodding his head towards me, indicating that he needed to talk.

"Go on in and I'll come find you in a minute." I kissed her on the lips, I didn't want to break apart but knew by the look on Drake's face that this was serious.

"Blade and Heather had to leave, Heather stumbled upon Uno and Ripped talking. They were talking about forming a merge with the Satan MC. They saw her, man. Blade got her out of there, told me to get the kids and girls here and tell the Prez to call a lockdown. He's afraid they'll come here."

"Shit. I'll get Prez to call church. You stay with the girls." We both hurried inside and I stormed into the Prez's office without knocking. "Shit!" I shouted as I crashed in to find Carla riding him in his office chair.

"What you doing? Get the fuck out, VP."

"I'm sorry, Prez, but we need to call church, now." Luckily Carla was still dressed and their connection was covered by the desk.

"Get everyone in the room and I'll be right there." I slammed the door behind me and could hear Carla screaming out as they finished what they had started. I got to the entrance of the bar.

"Church! Now!" I looked around and there was no sign of Cammie or Drake. "Where's Cam?" I asked Ashlyn.

"She's just trying to get the kids back to sleep. Are we on lockdown?"

"Yeah, sorry. Your guy will have to stay away for a bit."

"He's not mine. I mean, we're not a couple."

"Oh, really? He was here looking for you a couple of nights ago."

"Oh? Did he? Um…"

"No, I didn't see him with anyone else."

"Oh, um… I'm going to go and help Cammie." She walked away and I headed into church. We were waiting for Prez and ten minutes later he joined us with a shit eating grin on his face. Once he was sitting down, he slammed the gavel down and I announced that I need to call a lockdown. I explained the reasoning to everyone and they weren't happy but when it came to the ones we love, we would always join forces and protect each other.

Chapter 20

Cammie

"I got a couple of things I need to do, you gonna be ok with the kids?" Mason asked after I finished getting dressed.

"Yeah, can you just help me into the bar with them?" He nodded and picked up Liam. "Is Heather ok? I'm really worried about her. She wouldn't leave her kids, especially overnight if she didn't have to." Kelsey was staying with Ashlyn and they were already in the bar, she was sitting at a table with Prez's kids.

"They'll be fine. See you in a bit." He kissed me and disappeared off out of the clubhouse after placing Liam on Tat's lap, he was watching the news and Liam was happily gurgling away.

"You need me to feed him?" Ashlyn asked, pointing towards Liam.

"No, he woke up first so I already fed him," I explained as I got Tegan comfy and she reached for her bottle.

"You want a coffee?"

"Oh, yes please." I smiled.

"No worries." She wandered off towards the kitchen and I noticed that Drake followed her.

A couple of minutes later, I heard the main door fly open and Heather came running in.

"Mummy!" Kelsey called out and went running to her. Heather got ready to catch her and squeezed her tight. I could see their lips moving but couldn't hear what they were saying. Heather went for Liam next as Tegan was still eating, the excitement on his face was so amazing that it made me want to cry.

"Hi, sweet girl," Heather said to Tegan as she stroked the side of her face. Tegan stopped sucking and let out a cry. "Come here." I placed Tegan in her arms and she stopped crying and laid her head on Heather's shoulder. Heather smiled at me with thanks and I squeezed her hand in response. She would always be able to count on me.

***

I knocked gently on the door that Heather and Blade were staying in and pushed it open, popping my head in. Heather was laid on the double bed with the babies sleeping on the bed beside her.

"Hi." She smiled at me. I entered the room and looked around for Blade.

"Where's Blade?"

"He's gone to the Devon clubhouse." I stopped in my tracks, was I hearing her right? "I know, I didn't want him to go but he said he had to sort everything out once and for all." She looked back at the babies and once her eyes were focused on me again I could see tears welling. I trotted over to the bed and sat beside her and I grabbed her hand.

"I'm sure everything will be ok." I tried to soothe her.

"I'm scared, you saw what they did to him the last time, what if... What if he doesn't come back to us? I'm terrified of losing him." The tears rolled down her face and I wrapped my arms around her. I didn't know what to say, I didn't know if it was a good idea him going back but I also had a feeling he went as he didn't want them to be constantly looking over their shoulders for the rest of their lives.

"How long has he been gone?"

"A couple of hours." She picked up her phone from the

bedside table and glanced at it.

"I'm sure you'll hear from him soon." Just as I said that there was a knock at the door and Mason barged in followed by Solar and Ashlyn.

"Hey, babe," I said, looking at him. He stayed quiet and focused on Heather.

"We've gotta go. It's Blade." Heather and I both shot to our feet at the same time.

"What... What's happened?" Heathers voice shook as she asked the question.

"All I know is the clubhouse was blown up, we have to get to the hospital." Heather looked back at Liam and Tegan who were still fast asleep.

"I'll stay with them," Ashlyn said as she stepped forward. "Kelsey is with Carla."

Heather gripped hold of my hand, I squeezed hers back showing that I wouldn't be leaving her.

"Let's go," I urged.

We quickly exited the clubhouse and I jumped into the driver's seat of Heathers car, Mason and Solar climbed onto their bikes with Mason leading and Solar behind us. It was an hour and a half to the hospital he was taken to.

***

Once I had the car parked, we rushed into the reception and Heather asked for Blade; we were waiting for the nurse to find out the information.

"Heather." I tugged on her hand and when she looked at me I nodded my head to over her shoulder where Blade was standing. His clothes were black and dirty, his shoulder was in a sling and his face had cuts and bruises.

"Kade!" Heather called out as she went running towards him, she stopped just in front of him and he held out his good arm for her and she flung herself towards him. It was a relief to know that he was ok.

"You ok?" Mason asked as he stepped up beside me and placed his hand in mine. The warmth from his touch enveloped my body and I calmed down, seeing that Blade was ok was a relief.

"Yeah, I was scared then for a minute. What if she had lost him?"

"Then we would have helped her any way that we could." He placed a kiss on my cheek and I turned to face him.

"I'm glad to be home, I'm sorry we haven't had much time together since I've been back." I told him, turning to face him.

"I'm sure you'll find a way to make it up to me." He smiled, wiggling his eyebrows. "Come on." He pulled on my arm and we strolled over to Blade and Heather.

"You ok, man?" Mason asked.

"Yeah, just a dislocated shoulder and a few cuts and bruises. Wayne is in surgery, something about shrapnel lodged into his head or something. Sounded like they were talking in a different language." He tightened his grip around Heather and kissed the top of her head.

"I'm going to stay until Wayne is out of surgery, you go back with Mason and Cammie, sugar."

"But…" she started to protest.

"I'm fine, I'll be back in a couple of hours." He raised her head by her chin and kissed her. "I love you."

"Love you, too."

Heather and I got back to the car and made the journey home, Mason followed behind us on the bike and Solar stayed at the hospital so he could bring Blade back.

Chapter 21

Cammie

Blade and Heather had stayed with us for the past two weeks whilst he recuperated. I helped out with the kids and had a blast doing it, they were growing up so fast and I knew that I would miss them lots when they decided to go back to Devon. Blade had been voted as the new Prez for the Devon Destroyers MC and he had just purchased a rundown hotel on the outskirts of Devon. All the members were helping to restore it. It had three floors and the top floor was being converted into a home for Blade, Heather and the kids to live with a separate entrance at the back of the building so when the kids were older, they didn't have to go through the clubhouse to get to their home.

"You ok, babe?" Mason asked as he sat next to me on the swings in the children's playground.

"I just feel a little lost now, with Heather and the kids gone. I contacted Dan to see if the job was still available and he said it was mine if I wanted it. I start next week."

"Cammie," Mason complained.

"Please don't. I need to do this." I angled my body towards him and he was looking at me, smiling. He had on blue denim jeans, a white t-shirt and his leather cut, I could see the outline of his muscles on his chest and I wanted to run my tongue over them.

"I have a surprise for you."

"Do you?" My eyebrows rose and I smiled. "Gimme." I held out my hands for my gift.

"It won't fit in your hands, sweetheart." He chuckled.

"Oh. When do I get it?" I eagerly asked, I wasn't great with patience.

"Let's go now." He stood up and held his hand out for me. I quickly slipped mine into his and got to my feet, I loved surprises. I figured he was leading me towards the clubhouse but when we passed the door and was standing by his bike, I was confused. He passed me my helmet and I was about to push it onto my head when someone called his name. We looked behind us to see Titch standing there.

"I'll be quick," he said before he kissed me quickly and jogged over to where Titch was standing. I couldn't hear them but they looked like they were having a serious conversation. Once Titch disappeared, Mason hung his head and shook it like he had bad news. His hand searched in his pocket as he started making his way back towards me, he pulled out a cigarette and lit it. After only taking a couple of drags, he threw it on the floor and stomped it out, I rose my eyebrows in question.

"I'm trying to cut back." He laughed. "It's not working too well."

"Everything ok?" I asked as I placed my hand on his chest where his leather jacket opened, eager to feel his muscles.

"Yeah. Come on, I wanna show you your surprise." I stepped back as Mason swung his leg over the bike and got comfortable. I climbed on behind him, making sure I was nice and close. We took off out of the compound and down the road. I loved the feeling of riding with him, he was happiest on a bike and I loved that I got to share that with him.

***

We didn't travel far, only about ten minutes away from the clubhouse, we turned onto a street called Mulberry Drive. I wondered who we were visiting this time. The houses were small, looked like two floors, they all had driveways and a garden out the front and there were some kids playing football at the end of the road. It was a dead end, no way through. I would have loved to have grown up in a place like this. Mason pulled the bike onto the driveway and turned the engine off. I climbed off and removed my helmet, shaking my hair out.

"Who lives here?" I asked as he climbed off and placed his helmet and mine onto the bike seat. He gathered my hand in his and led me up the two steps that led onto the front porch. I tried to catch a glimpse in the living room window but I couldn't see anything. Mason used a key to get inside and I quickly followed him in, it was empty and bright as the sun shone through the house.

"Welcome home, baby," Mason whispered into my ear before kissing me on the cheek.

"What?" I asked as I took a step back. Was I hearing him right? Did he say welcome home?

"This house is all ours." He spread his arms out to the side and then leant against the banisters to the stairs.

"Oh my God!" I squealed running past him and into the kitchen at the end of the hall. The kitchen had patio doors that led to a large garden, a shed was sitting at the end next to a small pond and the patio area had a built in barbeque. The kitchen looked like it was brand new, the cupboards were cream with silver handles, a large stainless steel sink and a breakfast bar that had the oven built in to it. I looked up and Mason was standing in the doorway watching me.

"Are you being serious? Is this really all ours?"

"All ours, baby." He smiled. I ran up to him, kissed him quickly before I darted into the living room, it was a large room with a built in fire place. I could imagine loads of nights in here cuddled up in front of the fire with my kindle and my man.

"Wanna see our bedroom? Where we will be spending ninety five percent of our time?"

"Ninety five percent of our time?" I crossed my arms over my chest and looked at him.

"Hell yeah." He sauntered over to me, bent down and threw me over his shoulder.

"Mason, what are you doing, put me down." I laughed as he ran up the stairs, I was put on my feet once we were in the room. "Wow, this room..." I was speechless. We were standing in the doorway and in front of us was a large bedroom with two large windows, one had a window seat and the other led out to a small balcony. The view was breath taking, the sea stretched on for miles and it looked calm and peaceful. "It's beautiful," I sighed, feeling at home here already.

"It sure is." I turned my head as he spoke and noticed that he was looking at me, not at the view. I blushed slightly and he strolled towards me. "What's this?" he asked stroking my cheeks where I had blushed.

"I'm just not use to getting compliments," I quietly told him.

"Let me show you the en-suite."

"It has an en-suite?" I asked excitedly. He nodded and pulled me towards the door in the far corner of the room.

"Open it," he told me and I pushed the door open. The room was a lot bigger than I thought it would be. There was a large corner bath at the far end of the room, a walk in shower and a set of his and hers sinks.

"Oh, Mason, I love it." I threw my arms around his neck and kissed him on the underside of his jaw. We were moving again and I didn't complain, I loved how he could move me so easily with his strength.

"Here are the other two rooms." He placed me back on my

feet once again.

"Two rooms? This house doesn't look big enough outside to have three bedrooms." He opened the doors up and they were both decent sizes. We could easily get a double bed in both, these rooms would be prefect for Heather and the kids when they wanted to stay.

"Then we can extend over the garage if we need to." Extend? Why would need to extend this house is plenty big enough for the two of us.

"This is perfect for us two." I wound my arms around his waist and laid my head on his chest.

"And perfect for when we decide to fill the rooms with babies, though if we have more than two then we will have to extend, eventually."

"What? Babies?" I was stunned, speechless. He wanted kids? Why did I let it get this far? I should have been upfront with him and told him that we didn't have a future together if he was looking for a family. I couldn't go through that again.

"Mason, I didn't know that you wanted a family. I... I can't..." He cut me off.

"Yeah, at least a couple. I know you're too young at the minute. We have plenty of time. Want to see your other surprise?"

A couple? He wants at least a couple of kids? My face flushed, my heart battered against my chest and my stomach dropped. I was going to have to give him up, I couldn't move in here with him. We would be better if we parted ways now. How was I going to do that? Leave him? I stepped away from him, tears running down my face.

"Cam, what's wrong?" He palmed my face and looked into my eyes.

"I'm sorry, Mason. I can't live here with you."

"Don't give me that, you love the house, I just watched you

run about all excited. What's going on?" I pulled out of his grasp and took another step away.

"We're not meant to be together, this won't work. I don't want children. I can't give that to you Mason."

"Then we don't have children…"

"No, that's not fair on you. You just said you wanted at least two. You'll find that with someone else." I unzipped my leather jacket and went to take it off, to give it back to him.

"If you take that jacket off, so help me God, I will not be happy," he growled at me. "You love me Cammie, I know you do."

"Yes, I do love you, Mason, more than anything…"

"Shit." He cut me off as he pulled his ringing phone out of his pocket. "What?" He barked into the phone. "Fuck, I'll be right there." After he hung up, he looked at me. "I need to get back to the club." He grabbed hold of my hand as he walked past and I quietly followed him. Was this it? Were we going to part ways? My heart was breaking inside, would I actually be able to walk away from him? Could I have kids in order to keep him? The thought alone terrified me. I kept quiet as we rode back to the clubhouse, tears were silently streaming down my face. I looked up as we started to slow down, Drake started to open the gates for us to get through and the sight of the clubhouse, my home, made me cry even more. I was about to lose everything. As soon as the bike was parked, I jumped off and pulled my helmet off. As I walked by, I hung it on the handlebars and headed for the clubhouse doors.

"Cammie, wait!" Mason shouted. I ignored him and carried on. Should I leave straight away? Did we need to talk more? "Cammie," Mason growled as he gripped my forearm and spun me around. "Oh, baby." He enveloped me in his arms and I cried even more, clutching onto him. "I don't need to have a baby."

"Yes, you do…"

"I need you more, Cammie," he mumbled, cutting me off. I nuzzled my head into his chest and tried to memorise his smell, his touch and his love for me.

"No, you can't say that. I can't have you resenting me in the future because you never got the family you wanted."

"I don't understand, why don't you want children? You were great with Emily the other week?"

"I just don't. I love you, Mason, so much. It kills me to walk away from you but I'm not what you need or want." I unwound myself from him, stepped on my tiptoes and kissed him briefly on the lips. "Goodbye."

"No, you don't get to do that. You are everything to me, everything. I only want you in my life. I'm so in love with you, Cammie, I bought us a house to grow old in together…"

"You bought it?" I was stunned, I thought we would be renting it.

"Yes, because that's how much I love you. I never wanted to leave the clubhouse before, but with you I want so much more."

"But children…" I started.

"I don't need them like I do you."

"But…"

"Come with me." He took hold of my hand once again and strolled towards the back of the clubhouse. I had to trot along to keep up with his long strides.

"VP," Titch said nodding his head at Mason.

"Open the door," Mason demanded. I saw Titch look over his shoulder at me. "I said open the damn door." Titch jumped and his hands fiddled with the lock on the door before he pushed it open. Mason turned to me and placed his hands on my face.

"There's gonna be blood and shit in here, can you handle

that?" I nodded, not taking my eyes off his. He turned on his heel and led me into the room, the smell was eye watering; it was musty and foul smelling. I had to reach up to cover my nose. Mason led me over to two men tied in the middle of the room.

"Does this show you how much I love you? That I'd do anything for you?"

"Is that... Preppy?" He didn't look too good, his head was slumped forward and there was a pool of blood around him. "Is he dead?"

"Yeah, I'm afraid he bled out before we could have any fun with him. You need to trust in our love."

"Who's that?" I pointed to the other guy who was watching us. I stepped closer to him and recognised him instantly. "Screw." I remember him from the clubhouse, my stomach rolled and I thought I was going to throw up. He was always the guy that loved to tie us to a table so we couldn't move and then rape us.

"No, sweetheart, that's switch." I whipped my head around to look at him.

"That's not Switch, that's Screw. He's a Satan club member."

"What the fuck!" he roared. "Titch get in here, tell the Prez I need to call church, now!" While Mason's back was turned to me, I looked around for something I could use as a weapon, I wanted to hurt this man, inflict pain on him. There was a table nearby with some knives on it. Perfect. I grabbed one and threw it at Screw quickly before Mason saw what I was doing. I threw one after another until I got the area I was aiming for. He screamed out and Mason looked over his shoulder, he started laughing when he saw what I had done. There was a knife sticking out from Screw's crotch.

"He won't be using that again." I wiped my hands on my jeans trying to get rid of the grime that was on the knives but it didn't work.

"Let's get you out of here, sweetheart." He slung his arm over my shoulder and we walked away listening to Screw screaming about leaving the knife in his junk.

Chapter 22

Mason

We had a new plan, Titch and Toes were going to use their torture techniques to try and get Screw to talk and I was going to be heading over to the Pirates MC to find out why we were given the wrong Intel. That sick bastard that tortured my Cammie was still out there and he needed to be dead.

A drink was definitely needed and the Prez called a last minute party, he could see that we all needed to unwind; it was a party for the locals too. I didn't know what the situation between me and Cammie was; would she stay? Had she already left?

I walked into the bar and searched for Cammie, she was nowhere to be seen. I turned on my heel and headed for our room. If she had left, I would be tracking her down and dragging her here kicking and screaming if I needed to.

"Cam?" I called out as I entered the room to see she wasn't there.

"Yeah?" She was in the bathroom, I pushed the door open and she was looking in the mirror putting make-up on. I stood still and just watched her. After a couple of minutes of not talking, she stopped what she was doing and angled her head towards me. "You ok?"

"You didn't leave?" I exhaled, relief coursing through my body.

"No, should I have?" She frowned.

"You threatened too." I reached up and grabbed the door frame of the bathroom, causing my cut and t-shirt to rise up. I could see her eyes zone in on that part of my body almost instantly.

"I don't want to leave you, Mason." She sighed. "Maybe I'll feel differently about a baby in the future, I don't know. But at the moment, I can't promise you we'll have one. I'm sorry." She looked down at her hands fiddling with her make-up. I stalked into the room and stood in front of her. I waited until her eyes met mine.

"I'll be happy if it's just me and you, forever. Oh and a dog."

"A dog? We're getting a dog?" Her eyes lit up and I loved that I could do that to her.

"Yes. Company for you when we're on runs. What puppy would you like?"

"Oh, can we go to the rescue home and get one? I hate that the dogs are living in there."

"For you, anything. Shall I wait for you? Or meet you in the bar?"

"I'll be out in a little minute. I think I'll have rum and coke tonight please."

"You got it." I saluted her, she giggled and then I kissed her until we were both breathless. "Or we could just stay here?" I mumbled, not wanting to take my lips off of hers.

"You're the VP you have to show your face." I rolled my eyes, straightened my t-shirt and walked out of the bathroom. "A change of shirt wouldn't hurt either!" she shouted after me. I laughed out loud at her subtle way of telling me to change. I stripped off my cut and t-shirt and stood bare chested in front of the wardrobe deciding which shirt to wear; I went to grab the black one.

"The blue one would look better," she murmured behind me, then her lips touched my bare skin and she trailed kisses down my spine. My body shivered under her touch and my cock started coming to life. I looked at her over my shoulder and she was standing there in a pair of black skinny jeans, sparkly heels, a tight red top, her leather jacket and bright red lips.

"Is that stuff on my back now?" I ran the tip of my finger over her bottom lip and her tongue darted out.

"Yes. Just think of it as my mark on you."

"I like that." I slipped the shirt on over my head and proceeded to button it up. Pulling my jacket back on, we walked towards the party hand in hand. "I'll get us a drink." I leant down to kiss her and she threaded her fingers into my hair and deepened the kiss, if no one saw that she was wearing my properties they would soon know she was mine. My fingers bit into the skin on her hips and I wanted to be driving myself deep inside of her. I groaned once we separated.

"You've woken the beast now."

"Oh good, maybe he can come out and play tonight?" She licked her bottom lip and I had visions of my rock hard cock slipping through them.

"You can count on it." I slapped her ass gently as I walked away.

Cammie

I walked further into the room, saying hi to the members and the locals. I looked for somewhere to sit so Mason and I could enjoy an evening together without a care in the world. I stopped dead in my tracks when a familiar face was in front of me. What was he doing here?

"Dad?" I asked, unsure if I was seeing things correctly.

"Oh my God, Cammie, you're here." He stormed towards me and pulled me in tight to his chest. Not once in the last fifteen years had my dad had a reaction to me like this. I stepped out of his hold and looked at him. He had stubble covering his face and his clothes looked dirty and worn.

"What are you doing here? Where's mum?" I found myself looking around for her, was she here?

"She's not here. We've come to take you home." We've? Who the hell was he talking about?

"We?" I frowned, confused. "I am home. I'm not going anywhere."

"Cammie," his gravelly voice said and I froze. I turned my head to the right where he had spoken from. Was this really happening? Was he really here?

"W… What are you doing here?" I stuttered. I flinched as he moved closer towards me.

"Now, is that anyway to greet your boyfriend?" Dad said.

"Boyfriend? I haven't seen him for three years. He left me alone when I needed him the most!" I shouted.

"We're here to take you home," Jack said as he placed his hand high on my arm and gripped me.

"Here to take you away from these men. You don't need to be scared, they won't stop us." I tried to yank my arm away from Jack and his grip tightened. I screamed out and before I knew it Mason was flying across the room and Jack was laying on the floor. He pulled me into his chest and I gripped his back tightly, I didn't want him to let me go.

"Get your hands off her. She's mine!" Jack shouted at Mason. Mason's arms tensed and I kissed him on the chest, trying to soothe him. I wiggled my way out of his grip and turned to face my dad and Jack. With the back-up of Mason behind me, I found my strength.

"I'm not yours," I sneered at him. "I haven't been yours since you left me bleeding at the bottom of those steps three years ago." Mason placed his hands on my hips and his warmth made me feel safe and secure. I hadn't told him about this yet.

"And dad, I am home. All of these people care about me, I'm

not just someone who is in the way. I'm in love with Mason and won't be leaving him. You're not welcome here, please leave."

"What about us, Cammie? What about Noah?" Jack said.

"Don't you dare!" I screamed. "You have no right to say his name." I lunged for him and Mason held me back. Tears were clogging my eyes and when I blinked they began a trail down my face.

"He was my son too!" he snapped. The clubhouse went quiet and all eyes were on us. Solar, Tat, Drake and Ashlyn walked closer towards us. These were my closest friends and they were about to find out about my past.

"No! No, you don't get to call him that. You left us, you wasn't there when I had to give birth to him even though he was already dead. He wasn't breathing, Jack, it was because of the trauma I suffered when you let me fall down those stairs. I had to bury him, you were nowhere to be found."

"Cammie, I thought you hated me. Your dad contacted me and told me about Noah. I didn't know."

"I do hate you, Jack. I hate that you left me at the bottom of those stairs, I hate the fact that I had to bury my son alone. I hate the fact that I don't hate you for getting me pregnant. I had a couple hours with him to say goodbye and he was the best thing that ever happened to me. He was perfect." My crying had become frantic sobs as I fell to the floor, my heart was breaking all over again. I was losing him all over again, I couldn't cope with the pain. Darkness would find me and this time I wouldn't be strong enough to pull myself out of it.

"Get them out of here!" Mason yelled. "If you come back, I'll kill you myself," he threatened. My tears were coming thick and fast and I couldn't see anything.

"Cammie," Ashlyn said.

"I've got her." Mason picked me up off the floor and I curled into him. My head was banging from the crying but I couldn't seem to stop them falling. "It's ok baby, I've got you."

Chapter 23

Mason

I kept Cammie close to me, I obviously didn't know the shit she had gone through at such a young age. She'd had a baby, maybe that was why she was so adamant she didn't want kids now. I could never imagine having to say goodbye to a baby. Once I was in our room, I kicked the door closed behind me and sat down on the sofa with Cammie still clutched to me. I didn't want to let her go but I needed to talk to her about what was going on.

"Cam?" She shook her head and buried her face into my chest, her crying had eased but her body was still trembling. "Please, talk to me."

"I… I can't."

"Why didn't you tell me?" She all of a sudden sat up and looked at me.

"Can we go to our house? Please?"

"There's no furniture there, no electric, no heating."

"I just want it to be me and you, in our home."

"Ok, let me grab some supplies and we'll head over there." I went to lift her off my lap and she placed her hand on the side of my face.

"Thank you. I love you, I hope you know that."

"I love you too."

I searched through the storage cupboard in the hall for the blow up bed, sleeping bag, wind up torch and a battery operated heater. I was lucky that I found it as it was all in the back of the cupboard. I checked it all and it was working perfectly. I also found a box of tea light candles. I headed back to our room and heard that Cammie was in the shower, I left her to it and headed back into the bar to find Ashlyn. I dropped all of the stuff I needed by the front door, I needed to borrow her car.

"Holes," Ashlyn said behind me. I spun around and she had a trail of mascara on her cheek, I reached over and wiped it away. "How is she?"

"To be honest, I don't know. We're headed out for the night, can I borrow your car?"

"Sure, the keys are in it. Did you know about the baby?"

"No, did you?" She shook her head. "I'm hoping she will talk about it tonight. Can you make sure the guys don't ask her about it?"

"Of course."

"Thank you. We'll be back in the morning with the car." She smiled at me, gave me a hug and made her way to the bar.

"She ok, man?" Solar asked, gripping hold of my shoulder.

"She will be."

"That's gotta be rough." He exhaled and shook his head.

"Yeah. I'm gonna get back to her."

"Tell her we all love her, man." I nodded my head. Cammie and I were both lucky to have a family like this, brothers that would back you up and not turn your back on anyone.

I walked over to Ashlyn's car and stowed all the goodies I found in the boot, it would be a nice surprise for Cammie when she saw what I was up to.

I headed back to our room and I walked in to find Cammie curled up on our bed, she had something in her hand.

"What's that?" I asked, sitting on the edge and placing my hand on her back. She passed it to me and I was looking at a piece of paper with a tiny footprint on it.

"That's Noah's footprint. It's all I have of him."

"You don't have a photo?" She shook her head. Her wet hair

was piled on top of her head and my fingers itched to be able to run my hands through it.

"No, after he was taken away from me, I checked my phone, looking for the picture and it didn't take." Tears started to run down her cheek again and she frantically began wiping them away.

"You ready to go?" She nodded and I pulled her to her feet. She was dressed in a pair of grey leggings and an oversized hoody and on closer inspection it was one of my hoodies, I loved looking at her in my clothing.

***

As we pulled into the driveway to our house Cammie's phone started ringing. She looked at it and smiled.

"It's Heather."

"Answer it and come inside when you're ready." I kissed her on the cheek and she pressed the green button on the phone and held it up to her ear. I gathered all the stuff from the boot of the car and headed inside. I decided to set up the blow up bed in the living room, luckily it had a battery operated pump. As it was inflating, I spread the lit tea light candles on the hearth at the front of the fireplace and a few along the mantle. I uncorked the bottle of white wine and placed the two plastic cups with it. Once the bed was inflated, I spread the double sleeping bag over the top and turned on the battery operated heater. I didn't think it would last long, but it would be enough to take the chill out of the air.

"What's all this?" Cammie asked as she stood in the doorway to the living room. I had removed my jeans and leather cut. I walked towards her in my blue boxers, blue shirt and white socks.

"This is our first night in our home, I wanted it to be special." I reached out for her hand and she followed me into the room.

We got comfy on the bed, Cammie sat crossed legged beside me as I poured some wine into the plastic cups. I passed her one and the electricity zapped between us when our hands brushed together, she smiled slightly, looking into my eyes.

"To the first night in our new home," I said as I raised my cup towards hers. She did the same and we sat silently sipping our wine. It tasted like shit really, but I knew she liked it.

I laid back on the bed with my left arm under my head and crossing my ankles. Cammie sighed, I knew she was thinking about what happened earlier and I didn't want to push her to talk about it but also I needed to know, I wanted to know. She scooted closer to me and laid down with her head on my stomach, I pulled the tie out of her hair and ran my fingers through it, gently massaging her scalp. She clasped her hands together, moving her fingers almost nervously.

"When I found out I was pregnant, I was scared. I was only sixteen and my mum and dad weren't overly happy." She took a deep breath and I stayed quiet, not wanting to interrupt her. "I left after I'd told them and moved in with Jack, I thought we were happy until I came home from work early to find him and his roommates having a party and he was kissing someone else." My hand tensed and stilled in her hair. I watched as she placed both of her hands on her flat tummy. "The movements from him were breath taking, I cherished every one. Anyway, I left the flat and Jack followed me. He had hold of the top of my arm, much like the way he gripped hold of me tonight. I pulled away from him and he released his grip, causing me to fall down a flight of stairs. I tried to protect him, I wrapped my arms around my large tummy; I didn't want him to be hurt. I remember feeling the pain and not being able to move when I was laying on the floor at the bottom of the steps, thinking that I'd be ok as Jack would come and help me. I don't know how long I was there for, he never came. One of the neighbours found me and called an ambulance, I was… bleeding, God, there was so much blood." Her voice caught in her throat.

"Miss, how far along are you in your pregnancy?" the paramedic asked.

"Eight months." I cried out from the pain. "Please, please help my son."

"The pain was horrible, it felt like someone was sticking daggers in my back, and I prayed. I've never prayed before, but I prayed and begged that he would be ok. I already loved him so much."

"What's going on? What's happening?" I asked frantically as the nurses flitted around me in the hospital room. I had a strap along my belly and the nurse was looking at the monitor, she looked at the other dark haired nurse and subtly shook her head.

"We just need to check on the baby," she said as she squirted gel on my tummy and angled the monitor so I couldn't see. Usually, at my other appointments, I would be able to hear his heart beating and see him, why were they not letting me see?

"Is he ok? Why can't I hear his heart beating?"

"Is there someone we can call for you? I see on your records you are only seventeen. You should have a parent or guardian with you," a different nurse said.

"My mum is my next of kin," I told her. I didn't really want her with me but I understood they had a job to do.

I noticed the glances the nurses gave each other but no one was telling me anything.

"Please, is he ok? I can't feel him moving."

"The moment they told me that he had died…" She reached up and wiped her hand over her face. "I'll never feel pain like that again, I couldn't protect him and I couldn't save him. They said that when I fell, the placenta separated from the wall of my uterus; the placenta supplies the oxygen. He… he suffocated, if only I didn't leave that party, if only I didn't leave work early, he may still be here. I'd still be a mum." Her sobs became louder. I sat us both up and gathered her in my arms.

"You are a mum, you will always be a mum and you'll always have a son."

"And then they told me I still had to give birth to him, that it was important for my body to still go through that."

"Cammie, are you ready?" the nurse asked me as she pushed my legs up. "When you feel the contraction you need to push." They had given me a drug that induced labour. I had been waiting for it to start for the last four hours.

"No." I shook my head. "I can't do it. I felt him move, I know I did."

"Cammie, sweetie, I'm here to help you. It's time to meet my beautiful grandson." Mum gripped hold of my hand and I felt the need to start pushing. I opted out of having any pain medication, I needed to feel every inch of pain, no matter how much it hurt. That was my punishment for letting my son die.

"I pushed and I pushed. He was only four pounds when he was born, he was small but he was perfect." We had sunk back down onto the bed and her head was now resting on my chest and I trailed my hand up and down her back. She smiled when she remembered him.

"Do you want to hold him?" the nurse asked after she bundled him up in a blue blanket and blue hat. I held my arms out for him and nodded my head. He was my son, I needed to see him, to hold him, to love him. Once he was placed in my arms, it took me a couple of seconds to build up the courage to look at him.

"He's gorgeous, Cammie. Looks just like you did when you were born." Mum smiled. I gazed at him, he was perfect amd he looked like he was sleeping.

"I don't know how long I held him for. They let me dress him in a little blue onesie after doing his footprint."

"Cammie, it's time," Mum said as she walked back into my room

followed by a nurse. I knew what she meant, it was time for me to give him up. I held him up against my chest, kissed his head, told him that I loved him and that I always would.

"Then the nurse took him away from me. My heart broke when they told me he died, then it healed only slightly when I got to hold him, but the pain was excruciating when I watched her take him away from me. I felt like I was going to die, I couldn't breathe. A part of me will always be with him. That's... That's why I don't want children, I couldn't bare it if something like that happened again. I wouldn't survive it, I know I wouldn't." Her grip tightened on my shirt and I held her closer to me as she cried. A tear escaped from my eye and rolled down the side of my face, I couldn't stand seeing her so upset, I'd give anything to make everything better for her. We didn't speak, we just held each other and within a few minutes I could hear Cammie's breathing change, she had fallen asleep. I gathered the sleeping bag that we had managed to kick down the bottom of the bed and covered us both up. I would make sure she never felt upset like this again for as long as I lived.

Chapter 24

Cammie

I had kept myself busy for the last two weeks, I focused all my attention on decorating and furnishing our new home with the help from Ashlyn. I started working at the beach last week and it was fun, I enjoyed chatting with the people who wanted ice creams and beach supplies. Now we were getting into the start of summer the beach was getting busier which meant that I could work more.

"Cam?" Mason called out as he walked in the front door of our new house, tonight was going to be the first night of the rest of our lives and although I liked living at the clubhouse, being here just felt right.

"In the kitchen." I looked up when I felt his presence. I was chopping vegetables and throwing them into the slow cooker along with the chicken.

"You look good here." He smiled. "You've done a great job decorating." In the kitchen we now had a pine table and chairs, black kettle and toaster set and black and white spotted tea, coffee and sugar canisters. "You almost done?" He nodded towards the slow cooker.

"Yeah, that's the last of it."

"Good." He stalked into the kitchen as I washed my hands and gathered the dirty knife and chopping board and placed them in the dishwasher. I felt him close behind me and I leant back against him as he moved my hair off my neck and draped it over one shoulder. His stubble tickled me and I giggled.

"I've got a surprise for you," he whispered in my ear, the heat from his breath sending goose bumps all over my body.

"Oh yeah, is it this?" I moved my ass onto his growing cock and he moaned behind me, clamping his hands down onto my hips.

"It wasn't." He groaned and spun me around and slammed his mouth onto mine. Our kiss was heated and it was like we hadn't seen each other for a week, our teeth clashed and our hands collided as we attempted to rid each other of our clothes. Once Mason had my leggings and underwear down my legs, he picked me up and placed me onto the kitchen worktop; this way I was the same height as him. I fumbled with the tie on his shorts and once it released I slipped my hand inside and pressed my fingers onto his barbell piercings, his breath hissed out and I ran my hand up until I could flick the Prince Albert piercing too. I used my feet to push his shorts and boxers down until they fell to the floor. I had already managed to pull his t-shirt off, his chest was glistening with sweat after his run, he yanked at my hips until I was almost hanging off the side and I placed my hand behind me to balance, he entered me in one swift movement and I cried out, clutching my free hand onto his shoulder. He stilled his movements and gathered the bottom of my t-shirt into his hands and ripped it off over my head causing me to wrap my legs around his waist for balance as both of my arms were in the air.

"Fuck, you're so sexy. You ready, sweetheart?" I nodded and he unwound my legs from around him and hooked an arm under each one, spreading me. He used his hands to hold onto my ass and he pulled me towards him at the same time as thrusting into me. The sound of our body parts slapping together made me wetter and I loved how he took control of my body. Both of my hands were behind me, flat on the worktop causing my breasts to stick out as my back arched.

"I fucking love watching your tits bounce," he panted as he picked up his speed. "Come on, Cammie, let go." I reached one hand up and palmed my breast, they were both aching and one squeeze of my nipple had my walls clamping down, I threw my head back as I screamed out as the orgasm took over my body. I looked up immediately when I felt Mason pull away to see that he hadn't been wearing a condom and his release covered my body.

"You like making a mess." I laughed.

"Once your lips touch mine I forget who the fuck I am, let alone remembering to wear a condom." He shook his head. "I've never forgot before. Let's go get you cleaned up." He reached down for his boxers and shorts and pulled them back on. He grabbed a piece of kitchen roll and wiped me clean. After throwing it in the bin, he picked me up and walked upstairs to our en-suite bathroom, he placed me in the shower and turned it on. I stood under the heat and watched as he rid himself of his clothes and joined me.

***

We climbed into the car that Mason had bought me, it was a black BMW; it had only had one previous owner and was kept in great condition. He always insisted on driving when we were together.

"Where are we going? Why aren't we on the bike?" I angled my body towards his, I loved watching him drive, I loved the concentration on his face and the way his muscles flexed when he changed gear.

"It's a surprise, we will be there in a minute." He reached over and placed his hand on my leg, giving it a gentle squeeze. I closed my eyes and leant my head back against the headrest, I loved days like this, just Mason and I.

When I felt the car slowing down, I opened my eyes and

bounced in my seat to see we were at Southwest Dogs Home.

"Am I getting a dog?" I asked excitedly.

"We're getting a dog," he corrected me. We both got out of the car and made our way through the main entrance. There was a desk off to the right hand side and a path on the left that led to all of the dogs. Mason released my hand and walked to the desk.

"Hi, I called earlier…" His voice faded as I walked away from him and down the path toward the kennels the dogs were in. I stopped at each one, reading the info on the front.

"Lacey, a one year old Westie," I read aloud. I bent down and stuck my hand through the bars, she licked my hand and was so excited. How was I going to pick just one? It said on her kennel that she would need regular grooming, I needed someone a little less high maintenance.

"Hi, Bruno," I said as I stroked the top of the head of a Basset Hound. He was excitable and only six months old.

"Hello, Candy," I cooed as I let the four year old Pomeranian lick my hand.

"Hi, Dyson," I called out as the large black Rottweiler sat at the back of his cage, trembling. "Come here, boy." I tried to coax him over to me, his ears pricked as he listened to me. I sat on the floor and placed my hand inside his kennel. "Come on, let me stroke you." I wiggled my fingers and he stood on shaky legs and slowly made his way towards me. I knew that I shouldn't so willingly have my hand inside his kennel but he looked scared and frightened, I wanted to comfort him. I let out a light giggle when he nuzzled my hand with his nose, and I fell in love with him.

"Cammie?" Mason called out, I looked to my right and he was walking towards me with a small dog in his arms. I didn't take my hand off of Dyson.

"Who's that?" I asked.

"This is Dusty, she's a two year old Papillion. I saw her on the website and thought she would be perfect to keep you company when I'm away. They reserved her for us." She was cute and small, she would be a proper lap dog and I loved the long hair hanging from her ears.

"Oh," I said feeling disappointed and looking back at Dyson. He hung his head like he knew he wasn't coming home with me and my heart broke for him. "Can we get two?"

"I don't know if they will get on." Mason looked into the kennel and then read the information about Dyson. "Babe, he's already eight."

"Exactly, I want him to have a couple years of happiness." I was holding out hope that he would say yes.

"We could put Dusty back and just get Dyson," he told me.

"No!" I stood up abruptly. "Please, don't make me choose." I gripped hold of his free hand and squeezed it.

"Let me see what I can do, at least he looks fierce." He pointed towards Dyson. My heart soared at the prospect of getting two dogs. I wanted to take them all home really.

A couple of minutes later, Mason was walking back towards me with someone in a Southwest Dogs Home hoodie.

"Dyson has been here for nearly a year, he's not great with other dogs. I don't think it will possible to take both of them," she told me.

"Please can we try?" I begged.

"Ok, let's take them to the exercise area and see how they behave." She unclipped a dog lead from around her torso and unlocked Dyson's kennel. He sat at the back of the kennel in his bed.

"Come on boy. Dyson," I called out and his ears pricked up again. He slowly got to his feet and walked towards us. The woman clipped his lead up and I eagerly took it off her.

"Come on," I sung happily. We followed her towards the

exercise area.

"It'll be best to take him off the lead, then he won't feel restricted. He can't get out." I nodded and unclipped his lead. He didn't move, he sat next to my feet. I scratched the top of his head and Dusty barked happily in Mason's arms. He placed her on the floor and she bounded up to Dyson, he didn't take any notice of her and after she sniffed him she went off sniffing around the garden.

"Looks like they're good," I announced.

"They may be different when they are forced to live in the same house. We will fill out the foster paperwork and if everything is good in a month's time we can proceed with the adoption. Please don't hesitate to bring either one back if they don't get on."

"We will, I promise."

Mason followed the lady back to the reception and I stayed in the garden with the dogs, it was a nice sunny day and Dyson laid beside me as Dusty ran around. She was going to be the trouble maker out of the two of them.

Chapter 25

Mason

"You sure you're going to be ok here? You don't want to stay at the clubhouse?" I asked Cammie as she dished out the dog food. Dyson was laying on the floor by her feet and Dusty was bouncing around, barking.

"Babe, this is why we got them. Besides, Ashlyn is coming over later after I've finished work."

Dyson and Dusty had been living with us for three weeks and they got on great, they slept in the same bed and Dusty constantly followed him around the house and garden. I was heading out on a run with Solar and Tat, we were headed back to the Pirates MC. The Devil Descendants would be meeting us there and I needed to know why they gave us the wrong Intel on Switch. Toes had been trying to track him down and it was like he had disappeared off the face of the earth. Screw didn't give up any information even after hours of torture, he eventually bled out and the brothers had buried the bodies in the woods a couple miles away from the clubhouse.

"Call me or Prez if you need us." I dragged her into my arms after she had placed the dog bowls on the floor. "I don't know how long I'll be gone, I'm hoping only a day."

"We'll be fine." She placed her hands on my chest and looked up at me smiling.

"I love you."

"Love you too. Stay safe." I kissed her hard on the mouth not wanting to leave.

Solar and Tat followed me into the Pirates clubhouse, the Devil Descendants were already here. Their bikes were lined up outside.

"Here we go," I mumbled as we walked towards the bar, the Devils were sitting around a large circular table and the Pirates were gathered by the bar.

"So, what can we do for you VP?" The VP from the Devils asked, crossing his arms over his chest. I strolled towards him and placed my hands on the table getting close to him.

"I wanna know why the fuck you gave me false Intel!" I shouted.

"It's time I called in my favour." He smirked at me. "I gave you information, you said you owed me. Here's what I want… Him dead." He pointed at a picture before he pushed it closer to me.

"What the fuck! A cop! You want me to kill a fucking cop!" I roared and Tat and Solar had to pull me away.

"Calm down, brother," Tat said in my ear.

"I don't owe you shit! You gave us the wrong Intel and I'm still waiting to hear why."

"In that case, we'll just have to take you instead," he said as he nodded his head and two guys grabbed me, Tat and Solar were pinned up against a wall both with guns aimed at them.

"What the fuck!" I shouted.

"This is not what our clubhouse is used for!" the Pirates' Prez shouted. "We are the neutral ground, for compromising, not for this." He waved his arms around. I saw something out of the corner of my eye it looked like fire.

"Everybody out!" someone screamed.

"Petrol bomb!" someone else shouted. I was instantly released and we all fled the building as fast as we could. Tat and Solar were hot on my heels as we stormed out of the clubhouse to find shelter, we were blown off our feet as the Pirates' clubhouse exploded into flames.

***

Cammie

I had just finished my shift at the beach and looked up towards the clubhouse. I wondered if Mason was back yet. I decided to go and check. I had my car with me but it seemed silly to drive up there when it was a two minute walk across the beach. When I reached the back entrance to the clubhouse there was a commotion and I hurried inside to see what was going on. As I went to walk in, I noticed that Daisy and Titch were arguing on the cellar steps.

"What's going on? Daisy are you ok?" I touched her gently on the arm and she recoiled from me. She had dark bags under her eyes, her blonde hair was dirty and limply hanging around her face. Her jeans and t-shirt were crumpled and smelly. I hadn't seen her around the clubhouse for a little while and I felt bad that I hadn't tried to find out why.

"Do you want me to call Heather?" She didn't answer me, she kept her focus on the door Titch was blocking.

"I caught her trying to get in, no one is supposed to go in here," he explained to me.

"Daisy, why don't we go and get you cleaned up?" I softly spoke.

"Leave me alone! Leave me alone! Everyone leave me alone!" she screamed over and over again.

***

Mason

Shit, that explosion knocked me on my ass.

"Everyone ok?" I asked, looking at Tat and Solar.

"Yeah," Tat answered rubbing his fingers over the back of his head.

"What the fuck was that?" Solar complained.

I looked around and the Devils MC looked like they had already left, their bikes were missing.

"We need to check on everyone else." I stood to my feet, groaning in the process. The clubhouse was still on fire and I could hear sirens in the distance.

"Shit, we need to get out of here. Cops could be coming too!" Solar exclaimed.

"Fuck!" I cursed. I hated leaving the club without helping but my priority was my club and Old Lady. I wouldn't be any good to them behind bars. We climbed onto our bikes and drove out of the compound. Once we were a mile down the road, I saw a Harley Softail on the side of the road. I recognised it, but I couldn't put my finger on why or how. I pulled over to the side of the road, climbed off my bike and pulled my gun out. There was movements in the bushes and we all froze, drawing our guns and aiming at the movement.

"Holy shit! You fuckers scared me."

Cammie

Once Daisy had finished screaming, we heard another scream and it came from in the cellar.

"Is there someone in there?" I asked Titch.

"There shouldn't be." We heard the screaming again and it sounded like a woman.

"Open the door," I demanded. He hesitated. "Titch." He nodded and quickly fumbled with the locks.

"No, you can't go in there!" Daisy objected. We both ignored her and carried on through.

"I can't see a thing, is there a light switch somewhere?" I asked Titch.

"Yeah." I could hear him searching for the switch and once it turned on I gasped at the sight in front of me.

"Please help me, please. Before she comes back." There was a woman lying on a dingy mattress, her hands were tied above her head to a pillar post. She had long blonde hair, her clothes were dirty and tattered, she had track marks up her arms from drug abuse and she looked to be about nine months pregnant. She didn't look more than about twenty years old.

"Everybody stay back!" Daisy screamed as she stood between the girl and us, pointing a gun. Her hands were shaking and Titch pushed me behind him.

"What's going on here, Daisy?" he asked calmly.

"Nothing, I need you to leave and forget what you saw." She tried to shoo us away with the motion of the gun and neither one of us moved.

"Who is she, Daisy? Why is she here?" I asked, not sure I wanted to know the answer. She stayed quiet. "She's having a baby, this isn't good for her."

"That's mine," she stated. "That's my baby!" she screamed. "She fucked my husband, that's his baby. So therefore it's my baby. It's all I have left of him!" She was screaming and waving the gun around. I didn't know what to do, the woman on the bed was crying and all I was thinking was that the stress could kill that baby, I needed to get Daisy away from her.

"Daisy, please, let her go," I pleaded.

"No! Nooooooo." she screamed even louder this time.

Mason

We entered the clubhouse through the front entrance and all

we heard was someone screaming. We all rushed to the back of the clubhouse and the brothers were standing in the doorway to the cellar.

"Out the way!" I demanded. I could hear Cammie's voice. Shit, I needed to get to her.

"Daisy!" She stopped and spun around to face us.

"Ryan?" she cried, not believing that he was standing there. She threw the gun on the floor and ran towards him. I watched the gun fall all in slow motion, the safety must have been off as when it hit the ground a shot fired and I heard Cammie scream.

"No!" I shouted as I dove for her. I grabbed her and searched her for a bullet wound.

"I'm ok, I'm ok. I wasn't hit," she reassured me. I looked behind her and saw Titch laying in a pool of blood.

"Shit!" I dropped onto the floor next to him looking for the wound. It looked like it was coming from his leg. "Where do you hurt?"

"Thigh." He coughed. I saw the patch of blood and the hole where the bullet went in so I ripped the rest of the leg on his jeans open. It was oozing blood, I threw off my cut and ripped my t-shirt off over my head so I could try and stop the bleeding.

"Cam, I need you to hold this here." She fell to her knees and held it in position. "Someone get me a doctor!" I yelled. I yanked at my belt on my jeans and fastened it around the top of his thigh as tight as I could.

"You're gonna be fine. Stay with us." Cammie kept saying to him.

"Doc is on his way!" Drake called out.

"Let's get him upstairs!" I shouted and Tat, Solar and Toes stepped forward to help carry him. "You got it, Cam?" She nodded as she concentrated on keeping pressure on his leg.

"One, two, three, lift."

"Aaahhhh," Titch complained.

"Don't be a pussy, chicks don't like that." Solar laughed.

"Yeah, think of all the attention you'll get from the scar." Tat joined in.

We managed to get him upstairs and onto his bed just in time for the doc to arrive. Ashlyn helped him as she had some nursing experience.

"Let's get cleaned up." I exhaled as I led Cammie into our bedroom.

"What about the girl?" she asked.

"Prez and Carla are sorting her out." We both stripped out of our clothes that were covered in blood and climbed into the hot shower. Luckily we decided to keep this room stocked with shower gel, shampoo and clothes as we knew sometimes we would be staying here.

"Who's that Ryan guy?"

"That's Daisy's husband." She stopped scrubbing her body and looked at me.

"I thought he died. I'm sure Drake told Heather that he had died."

"I don't know all the details yet, sweetheart. I need to get to church." She kissed me before I opened the door to the shower. I wrapped a towel around my waist leaving one out for Cammie before I quickly got changed and headed to church.

I walked in the door and everyone was sitting around the table including Ryan, whose club name was Hitch. Apparently, he has had several wives in the past. He was sitting in my VP chair, he was the last VP and I was promoted to that chair as I thought he had died.

"Hitch." Prez nodded at him to move and he stood up and moved down the table to the next free seat. The Prez slammed the gavel down. "First, Titch is going to be fine. Luckily, the bullet didn't hit anything major. He just lost some blood and the doc is getting him some more. Second, Hitch has been working undercover, he went to the Cardiff Carvers MC as a prospect. They have been the ones attacking the clubs down this way, the attack on the Pirates MC today was them. They are trying to gain territory, they think by taking out all of the Cornish clubs they can claim the southwest for themselves."

"Surely an undercover mission should be voted on?" Toes added.

"Normally, yes. We were hit by these guys, they tried to take us out when we were on a run. Hitch had head trauma and was in a coma. We had this pact, like I do with all of you. He didn't want Daisy to live on the hope that he'd recover, he wanted her to live her life, find someone else and be happy. When I got the call from the hospital weeks later that he was awake, he wanted revenge, he wanted to take this club down, he wanted to go undercover so we had the best chance of attacking them."

"Daisy already thought I had died, there was no good in telling her I survived to tell her I wasn't coming back, and she couldn't have gone with me."

"So what's the deal with this woman in the cellar?" I asked.

"I've spoken to Daisy, a while back we discovered that she couldn't have children, we were going to find a surrogate but that takes time and we wanted a family. We had a deal and we picked someone, I fucked her a few times and we were lucky enough that she got pregnant. That's the woman downstairs. Daisy said she has been watching her, she's a druggie. Daisy locked her up, thinking that she would be helping the baby."

"Shit," I cursed. "What now?" I focused on Prez.

"I rode with the Cardiff Carvers MC here, my plan was to

alert the Pirates MC but I couldn't. Before I left, I anonymously posted all the details to the future plots, runs and dealings to the police along with past ones. Hopefully they'll get picked up soon by the cops."

"Did they discover your ties here?" Prez asked him.

"No, I stayed at the clubhouse all the time. Never let them onto anything, I claimed I had no one and I was one hundred percent committed to them."

"Good work." Prez slammed the gavel down and we all filed out of the room. I needed a fucking drink. I headed towards the bar and before I sat on the stool Penny had a whiskey waiting for me. I grabbed it and downed it in one, hissing at the burning in the back of my throat.

"Where's Cammie?" I asked Ashlyn who was sitting at a table with Drake and Solar.

"She's with Titch." I nodded and walked away, heading for his room. I knocked once on the door and walked in. Cammie was sitting on the edge of his bed, holding his hand. She was in black leggings and my hoodie, her hair was tied up and she smiled at me as I entered. I saw Titch's wide eyes as he tried to retract his hand from Cammie's. She released it and held her hand out for me. I stood by the side of her.

"How you feeling?"

"Pretty good, the doc fixed me up with some strong pain killers."

"I heard you protected my girl?"

"He did, he made sure I was behind him when Daisy started waving the gun around and when the gun fell to the floor he pushed me out of the way."

"Thanks, man, I really appreciate it. You're good for this club. I'm gonna talk to Prez about getting you patched in early. No promises though."

"Thanks I really appreciate it." His words were slightly slurred and I could see he was getting tired.

"We'll let you sleep," Cammie said as she squeezed his hand once more. By the time we had reached the door, his eyes were closed and he was snoring. "Take me home." Cammie sighed as she leant in to my body.

"My pleasure." I tipped her chin up and kissed her.

Chapter 26

Cammie

I stretched my arms above my head as I woke up, I looked to my left and was disappointed to see that I was in bed alone. We had stayed at the clubhouse last night after the party, Ashlyn and I had drunk loads and danced most of the night. Titch was managing to get around a bit better now with the help of crutches and the bunnies all tried to help him in any way they could, I couldn't believe he was shot only a week ago. Hitch and Daisy were back together, she seemed like a completely different person than before and the girl who was carrying his baby was in a rehab centre, she wanted to get clean herself but couldn't afford to. The deal was that they would pay for her to get clean and she had to sign the baby over to him once it was born and she agreed.

I did a mental check before I attempted to get out of bed, yep my tongue felt fuzzy, my stomach churned and my head pounded. It was a great night. I forced myself out of bed so I could use the toilet, I breathed deeply as my stomach rolled. Was I going to be sick? I just needed something to settle my stomach and head.

I routed through the wooden set of drawers in the bathroom, looking for some paracetamol when I froze. I came across my tampons and realised that I hadn't needed them for a little while. Shit! What have I done? Could I be pregnant? I racked my brain trying to think back to when my last period was and for the life of me I couldn't remember. I admit we were not always great at using protection and I hadn't found time to get to the doctors to be put on the pill. Most of the time Mason would pull out, but even then, there's a massive risk. Fuck. Fuck. Fuck. How could I have let this happen? I needed to know. I stripped out of Mason's t-shirt that I was wearing and slipped on some jeans and a t-shirt, threw my hair into a pony tail, grabbed my bag and keys and ran towards my car.

"Cammie?" Ashlyn called out as I ran past. Shit, we were supposed to be having breakfast together. I couldn't think about that now. The nearest shop was only ten minutes away and then I'd be back. I waited impatiently while Drake opened up the gate for me, I wound my window down as he waved at me to stop.

"VP know you're heading out?" he asked.

"I won't be long. Couldn't find him this morning."

"Early morning business to attend to." I nodded my head, knowing that I shouldn't ask any questions. I just wanted to get out of there, I felt sick at the thought that I could be pregnant, especially after all the alcohol I drank last night. Surely, if I was pregnant, the baby wouldn't survive that. That thought alone made my stomach dip, I couldn't lose another baby, I just couldn't.

I quickly ran into the shop, bought a couple of pregnancy tests and headed back for the clubhouse.

"Wow, that was quick." Drake laughed as he opened the gates for me. I smiled at him, parked my car and ran back to our room. I was hoping that Ashlyn hadn't seen me coming back in.

I paced the small bathroom trying not to look at the pregnancy test that was laid out by the sink. What was I going to do if it was positive? I looked at the time on my phone again, it was time to look at it. I took a deep breath in and picked up the test – negative. I exhaled, relief coursing through my body and disappointment, did this mean I wanted to have a baby? These tests weren't always accurate so I decided to take the other one just in case. Those minutes were just as much agony as the last ones. When I picked up the test, my stomach dropped and I fell to my knees in front of the toilet, throwing up the food and drinks from last night. How was it positive? One negative and one positive? What did that mean? Shit! I closed the toilet seat and pulled the flush, I rinsed my mouth out and walked out into the bedroom to see Ashlyn standing there.

"You ok?" she asked, looking concerned. I shook my head as tears began running down my face. "What's happened?" She stalked towards me and wrapped me in her arms.

"One's negative and one's positive." I sobbed.

"What?" She pushed me back so she could look at me. "You took a pregnancy test?" I nodded.

"They're in the bathroom but they say something different on each one." I frantically tried wiping my tears away. She rushed into the bathroom and thirty seconds later, she appeared with them both in her hands.

"Um… Cam, they are both positive." She held them up to show me.

"What?" I took them off her. "How is that possible?" I looked at them and then dropped them onto the bedside table.

"Maybe you didn't wait long enough."

"Oh God," I cried, sitting on the edge of the bed and covering my face with my hands. I'm pregnant. Shit. Fuck. What was I going to do?

"Are you ok?" Ashlyn asked as she placed her hand on my back. I shot up off the bed, shaking my head.

"No. I drank so much last night. I don't even remember getting into bed. I've probably already killed my baby." I placed my hands on my tummy and prayed that this wasn't true. "I'd be a terrible mum, I was a terrible mum. I lost him, he was taken from me and I couldn't keep him alive. I'd lose this one too." I was pacing in my bedroom as tears kept falling down my face.

"You need to tell Holes."

"No. Not if the baby hasn't survived, I couldn't do that to him. He will never get to feel what it's like to lose a child. He'd never forgive me. I have to go." I grabbed my car keys and dashed out of the room, Ashlyn calling out my name behind me. I left everything else behind; my money and phone. I tapped my fingers impatiently on top of the steering wheel as I waited for Drake to open the gates. He leant down to talk to me again and I didn't stop, I pushed my foot on the accelerator and shot away. I looked in my rear view mirror as I heard the roar of bikes, praying that Mason didn't see my car driving away.

***

I pulled my car up outside of Heather and Blade's house. Her car wasn't here but maybe I'd be lucky and she would be in. I pulled down the sun visor to look at my reflection in the small mirror, my eyes were red and puffy. There was no hiding the fact that I had been crying and she would have seen right through me anyway, I couldn't keep anything away from her. I rushed up to the door and rung the door bell, no answer. I tried the door handle and it was locked. Shit. I'd try the clubhouse, if I could find it. Heather had explained where it was located and surprisingly it was easy to find.

I stopped by the prospect who was by the gates, I didn't recognise him so he must have been new.

"What can I do for you, sweetness? You lost?" He smirked, the corner of his lips rising. In my rush to get out I forgot to put on my properties.

"I'm here to see Heather, I'm Cammie."

"Does she know you're coming?" I shook my head. "Sorry,

babe. I can't let you in."

"Is Blade here?" He shook his head. "Riz? Itch?" He shook his head. I covered my eyes with my hands, leaning my elbows on the steering wheel, what was I going to do?

"Hold on, let me call the VP." He walked over to his little hut and I could see his lips moving but couldn't hear the conversation he was having. His head rose and he looked at me, smiling. "You can go on in!" he shouted as he pushed the gates open. I sighed in relief. When I rounded the corner and parked my car in the small parking area there was a guy with a shaved head leaning against the wall. I looked up to the old hotel and it didn't look liveable, maybe the inside was better.

"Hey, Cammie." He lifted his head and smiled at me.

"Wayne?" I asked, walking towards him.

"Buzz is the name now," he said as he scratched his fingers over his shaved head.

"Sorry."

"You looking for Heather?" I nodded. "She's dropping the kids at nursery, she won't be long. You wanna wait inside?" I shook my head. I wasn't wearing my properties and I was a club whore for this club several months back, I didn't want anyone thinking that was what I was there for. "If you head around the side of the building, there is a black door, that's the entrance to Heather and Blade's place. You can wait there."

"Thank you." I smiled and headed in the direction he told me. I sat on the bottom step, pulled my legs up to my chest and placed my forehead on my knees and let the tears fall. I didn't know how I was going to do this, I'd be a wreck, always panicking that something was wrong.

"Cammie?" I looked up to see Heather standing in front of me, her smile dropped from her face when she saw the look on mine. Her wavy brown hair blew in the slight breeze and she rushed towards me. "What's wrong? What's happened?"

"I…" I shook my head, I couldn't say the words, not again. I placed my hand on my tummy hoping she'd get what I was saying.

"Ahhh!" she screamed happily. "You're pregnant?" She grabbed my arm and pulled me to stand up so she could hug me and as soon as her arms were around me, I lost it and cried. "Hey, what's all this? You not happy about it?" I shrugged my shoulders. "Let's go upstairs. You'll have to excuse the mess, we're still trying to get this place liveable." She unlocked the black door and we walked up a flight of stairs to where there was another door, she unlocked that one and pushed it open. We came right into the living room, it was huge and the windows carried across the whole front of the building. To the left was the kitchen, then to the right there was a small hallway that I guessed led to the bedrooms.

"Wow, Heather, this is amazing." It was in the middle of being re-decorated, there was only fold up chairs to sit on and a kettle and mugs in the kitchen.

"It will be great once it's done. Kade will be on hand for the club but he won't have to stay away from us either. Now, come and sit down and talk to me."

We sat in the fold up chairs opposite each other and Heather reached forward and grabbed my hand.

"You don't want to have the baby?"

"I'd never get an abortion… I want the baby, I just don't want to be pregnant and I don't want to be responsible for keeping him or her alive. I've already failed at that once." A sob rose in my throat and I took a deep breath to try and calm myself down.

"Cammie, that wasn't your fault. That was the dickhead who let you fall down the stairs, he left you and didn't help you. You did everything right, your baby boy was healthy."

"I'm so scared," I whispered.

"I was scared, do you remember? When my waters broke, you delivered my son. You were calm and collected, you saved him." The sobs escaped, I acted calm but I was terrified that Liam wasn't going to be moving when Heather gave birth, I was terrified that it would take me back to the time and place when I looked at my son who looked like he was sleeping, but he wasn't breathing. He was cold and not moving. Then happiness soared through my body when Liam let out his first cry, clenching his fists. I didn't want Heather to experience what I went through, I wouldn't wish that upon my worst enemy.

"You can do this, you're strong enough. Besides you have me and Mason this time. We are here for you, always."

Chapter 27

Mason

I hated sneaking out of the clubhouse before Cammie was awake, she looked sexy as sin sleeping with sex crazed hair and in one of my t-shirts. I wanted to crawl under the covers and wake her up in a great way, an orgasm was always the best way to start the day.

I had a surprise for her and I wanted to get it sorted before she came home. I walked into our house and was greeted by barking dogs.

"Hi, you two. Come on, out in the garden." I tried to step around Dusty without stomping on her. They both shot out in the garden once the patio doors were open, I left the door ajar so they could come in and out as they pleased. It was a sunny morning and I enjoyed the sun on my face as a smoked the first cigarette of the day. I needed coffee too. I stepped back into the house and flicked the switch to the kettle on. While that was boiling, I put my plan into action. I moved the sofa to the back wall and placed the blow up bed in the middle of the room, I set out all the candles and the bottle of wine. This time I had it in an ice bucket as it was a warm day and I wasn't sure when she would be getting here.

Once my coffee was ready, I started drinking it as I set my next plan in motion. I closed the kitchen door to the hallway; the dogs would have to stay in there for a little while. I started spreading a trail of rose petals from the front door to the living room door, in the room and around the blow up bed. If any of the guys caught me doing this shit I'd be a laughing stock. I clearly didn't think this through very well as the fucking petals were sticking to my shoes.

I sat in the back garden with my coffee and cigarette number two, feeling nervous as hell. What if she hated it?

I'm at home. Get that sexy ass of yours here x

She should be here within the next ten minutes, when thirty minutes had passed and there was no sign of Cammie or a respond to my text I started to worry. I pressed my recent calls list on my phone and Cammie was at the top, I hit her name and listened to the phone ringing constantly until it went to voicemail. I tried three more times before I got fed up. I jumped to my feet and hurried the dogs inside, filling their bowls up with dog biscuits before I rushed to my bike and headed for the clubhouse.

Once my bike was parked, I marched into the clubhouse, stopping to look in the bar area for Cammie, there was no sign of her. Surely she wasn't still asleep. I pushed the door open and frowned when she wasn't in the bed, the shower wasn't on. Maybe she was doing her make-up? Was she working today?

"Cam?" No answer, I nudged the bathroom door open and it was also empty. I grabbed my phone out of my pocket and dialled her again. Still no fucking answer. I looked out of the bedroom window and couldn't see her car in the beach carpark. As I walked towards the door to find Ashlyn, something on the bedside table caught my eye, I strolled towards it to see what it was.

"Fuck!" I swore as I dropped to the bed and hung my head as my forearms rested on my thighs, still holding onto the pregnancy test. She must be freaking out somewhere. Where the fuck was she?

"Holes?" I looked up to see Ashlyn standing in the open doorway.

"Did you know about this?"

"Yeah, I came to find her for breakfast and she was in a bit of a state."

"Where is she?" I dropped the pregnancy stick back down and scrambled towards her.

"I don't know."

"You don't know? Why did you let her leave? Why didn't you call me?" I shouted.

"VP, calm down," Prez said as he entered the room. I took a step back from her and ran my hands through my hair.

"Where is she, Ashlyn?" I asked again, calmer this time.

"I don't know, I couldn't stop her. She left her phone and purse here."

"Fuck!" I roared as I stormed past them and out the door to my bike. I headed for the other place she may have been.

***

Cammie

"Sugar?" Blade called out as he walked in through the door. We both looked up at him and the worry on his face seemed to disappear. "Ah good, you're here. Holes is going crazy trying to find you."

"What?" I reached into my jeans pocket for my phone and realised I didn't have it. "Shit, I must have left my phone at the clubhouse. Is he mad?"

"He ain't happy, sweetheart." He leant against the doorframe and crossed his arms across his chest.

"I better get home." I stood up and carried my mug into the kitchen and dropped it into the sink.

"He's on the way here."

"Oh." I glanced at Heather and she stood up and stepped towards me.

"Everything is going to be fine. Talk to him, don't push him away and remember I'm here for you, always. Just call me and I'll be there."

"Thank you." She wrapped her arms around me once more and rubbed circles onto my back.

"Oh, babe, before I forget Daisy and Ryan are coming up in a couple of days to stay."

"Sugar, its Hitch. You have to use his club name." He sighed at her.

"He's family." She waved her hand like it was ok.

"Sugar," he said in a warning tone, raising one eyebrow.

"Fine. Hitch."

"Prez!" I gasped when I heard Mason's tone. He wasn't happy, not in the slightest.

"She's in here, VP." Blade moved to the side and I watched as Mason filled the doorway. As soon as his eyes connected with mine, his face softened.

"You ok?" he asked, shuffling into the room. I nodded and scrambled towards him, I wrapped my arms around his neck as he bent down to gather me in his arms. "I was worried about you," he whispered which made me tighten my grip on him. "So, we're having a baby?" I nodded. "Are you happy about it?"

"I'm scared," I admitted. He nodded his head in understanding.

"Let's get you home." He kissed me on the side of my head and we separated. I looked around and saw that Heather and Blade had left us alone. "You going to be ok to drive? Or shall I leave my bike here?"

"I'll be fine. I need to find Heather, I disrupted her day."

"Come on, sweetheart." He held my hand and we walked down the stairs, out of the door and around the corner to the clubhouse. "Where's your jacket?"

"I forgot to put it on this morning, I'm sorry."

We walked in through the front door and the inside was amazing, it looked just like a hotel. There was a large area in front of us, with a big room at the end, a grand staircase to the left and a dining area to the right.

"Hey there, handsome." A dark skinned girl with jet black hair, wearing only a pair of denim shorts a small tank top and heels said as she ran her hand over his chest.

"Anna," Heather said as she walked up to us. "Go and sort the bar out, will you?"

"Sure." She smiled to Heather and then turned to Mason. "Come and find me later, handsome. Once you're done with that one."

"Anna," Heather warned her. She looked at Heather as if to say she wasn't doing anything wrong. "This is the VP for the Cornish Crusaders." Her eyes lit up until Heather added, "And his Old Lady Cammie. My best friend." Her shoulders slumped and she scuttled away.

"You ok?" Heather asked me.

"Yeah, I'm sorry I bombarded you with this."

"Hey, you can always come to me. Promise me." When I hesitated, she said. "Cammie, promise me."

"I promise." We hugged, said our goodbyes and were soon driving home.

Mason

The look on Cammie's face when I walked into Heather and Blade's home wasn't a look I wanted to see again. She looked lost, upset, scared and I would do everything in my power to protect her and the baby.

Fuck, I was going to be a dad. That was some scary shit.

I waited by the front door for Cammie to climb out of her car and join me. I held her hand and unlocked the door, she gasped once she entered. Shit, I forgot about all of the rose petals. My plan was far from my mind when I couldn't find her.

"Shit, sorry. Just ignore all of that stuff, I'll get it cleaned up in a bit. Do you want to have a lie down?"

"No, I want to know what all this is for." She followed the trail that led into the living room and she stopped when she saw what I had done.

"I wanted to re-create our first night here, there was something I wanted to do."

"Oh and now you don't?" She seemed disappointed, I cradled her face in my hands and kissed her soft lips.

"I do, I really do."

"Wait." She used her hand to push me back slightly. "We can't have sex."

"We can't?" I asked, eyebrows raised high off my head. What the fuck was she talking about?

"No, what if we cause the placenta to detach?" She bit her bottom lip, eyes filling with tears.

"I'm sure that won't happen." She opened her mouth to speak and I placed my finger on his lips. "But we'll wait until we see a doctor, ok?" She nodded. "Come with me."

She followed behind me until she was sitting on the blow-up bed, I reached into her hair and pulled at the tie.

"Mason," she complained. "My hair's a mess." She began coming it through with her fingers.

"It's gorgeous, like you." I angled her face towards mine and brushed her lips with a sweet kiss until she parted her lips for me and I invaded her mouth, our tongues colliding together. My cock was starting to come to life and I had to break our connection before we got carried away. I grabbed the wine bottle out of the cooler and hurried out of the door, I was going to swap it for some sparkling grape juice, she had bottles of the stuff. I personally thought it tasted like shit, but she couldn't get enough of it. The dogs barked and jumped up at me as I entered, I unlocked the patio doors and opened it up for them. Dusty shot out into the garden while Dyson sat at the kitchen door sniffing underneath it.

"You can see mummy in a minute, dude," I told him and he angled his head to the side, pricking his ears up. I squeezed past him and strolled back into the living room, Cammie was now laying on the bed with both of her hand flat against her tummy.

"You ok?"

"I will be after I've seen the doctor. I'm going to call and make an appointment in a minute." I sat down at the side of her on the bed, which caused her to bounce around, those tits looked amazing.

"First, here." I passed her a plastic cup with some grape juice in it. "To us."

"To us." She giggled.

"Cammie, I'm so in love with you. From that first moment that I laid eyes on you at the clubhouse, I was fascinated by you. You were shy and quiet but I could see there was a feistiness about you. I love that you give me hell when we are alone and that you respect me and my club when we have company. You are the perfect fit for me and I never ever want to let you go." I slid off the bed and onto my knee, I felt like an idiot doing it this way, but she deserved the best and I wanted to give her everything that I could. I pulled the box out from my pocket and her eyes zeroed in on my hands.

"Cammie, will you marry me?" I opened the box and her mouth fell open to see the silver band with a large diamond nestled on top.

"Oh, Mason." She threw herself at me, which I wasn't expecting and we toppled to the floor, causing me to drop the ring. She slammed her lips down onto mine and I controlled the angled of her head by pulling on her hair.

"Is that a yes?" I mumbled against her lips. She pulled her head back and laughed.

"Yes, it's a yes. A thousand times yes!" She cried, happily.

"I dropped the ring."

"What?" She gasped as she pushed herself to her feet. "Where did you drop it?"

"In this area somewhere, I got distracted when this extremely hot twenty year old blonde threw herself at me." She slapped me on the stomach telling me shut up. She crawled around on the floor with her ass high up in the air looking for the ring and I had to adjust the not so little problem that I was having in my jeans.

"Oh, I found it." She showed me and then slipped it onto her finger. "It fits."

"Hey, I'm supposed to put it on your finger," I complained. I moved myself so that I was now leaning against the blow up bed with my arm keeping it in place. Cammie crawled over to me and climbed on top of me, straddling my thighs.

"I love you, Mason, I can't wait to be Cammie Cole. Hey, that's got a nice ring to it." I loved seeing her so happy, especially after this morning.

"Are you really ok?" I asked as I ran my hand up and down her side.

"I don't know. I'm really scared and I can't promise I won't be a nightmare through this whole pregnancy."

"Did you ever talk to anyone about what happened? A professional?"

"No, they suggested it at the hospital but we never looked into it. I never planned on any of this." She waved her hand around the room before settling it on my chest. "I never dreamed of having the perfect house, the perfect man or having any babies. I was just a club whore, you know?" I growled deep in my throat when she used that word. She wasn't a whore, she was mine. My Cammie, My Old Lady and soon, very soon, my wife.

"Do you want to talk to someone about it? I can be there with you if you want or not? Up to you."

"Um… I don't know. I wonder if it'll help my fears."

"We can ask the doctor when we go."

"Yes, good idea. I'm going to call them now." She pressed a quick kiss to my lips before she hurried out of the living room and into the kitchen. "Hi, babies." I heard her talking to the dogs. I stayed still for several minutes, wondering how quick I could get her to marry me.

Chapter 28

Cammie

"How did it go?" Ashlyn was upon us before we even got through the clubhouse door properly.

"It went great," I started to say when Mason kissed me on the side of my head and angled his head towards the church doors. I nodded in understanding, they had a meeting. "I can't believe it, I'm actually seventeen weeks pregnant, we can find out if we are having a boy or a girl in three weeks, but we are going to let it be a surprise."

"You look happy." We sat down on the sofa by the window.

"Yeah, I am. I'm still so scared though. We heard the heartbeat and it's good and strong. I haven't felt any movement yet though." I placed my hands on my tummy.

"Where did that bump come from? You didn't have that last week!"

"I know, it's crazy. It's like, all of a sudden it was there." I laughed.

"Hey, you ladies want a drink?" Drake asked placing his hand on Ashlyn's shoulder.

"I'm ok thanks," I answered and Ashlyn shook her head, not looking at him. "What was that? That was a frosty reception."

"Nothing. So, I hear VP wants to get married as soon as possible."

"Yeah, but he's got it in his head that I want a big wedding. I don't."

"Oh, I saw this post on Pinterest." Ashlyn said digging her phone out of her pocket and showing me. "It could be done here, they have that large area right at the back of the clubhouse."

"I love that idea. You'll be a bridesmaid, won't you?"

"Yes, of course."

"Will you come with me to Mason's mum's house? Let's get planning this wedding."

"Now?" she asked. I nodded and we climbed to our feet and made our way to the front door.

"Hey, where are you off to?" Mason asked as we were almost out the door.

"I'll wait outside," Ashlyn said, leaving Mason and I alone together. He stalked towards me and kissed me hungrily, pushing me gently against the wall and pinning my arms above my head.

"I need to be inside of you, a week is a long fucking time." We had spoken to the doctor about my concerns with sex and he assured me that it was perfectly safe and I had an appointment to see a counsellor next week too.

"Me and Ashlyn were just heading over to your mums."

"Why?" He looked confused. I loosened one hand from his grasp and ran it over his cheek and scratched his stubble on his jaw.

"I've decided on the wedding I want and we are going to start preparations so I can be your wife within the month."

"I fucking love that, but don't I get a say in how and where we get married? I want you to have everything you want."

"I will have everything I want in six months. A gorgeous husband and hopefully a healthy baby."

"Baby Cole is going to be perfect." He released my other hand and I played with the dark hair at the back of his neck. "I'll come with you and then we can tell her about the baby too. But tonight, I'm going to be balls deep in my fiancée."

"I can't wait." I kissed him once more before he pulled away.

Mason

I fucking loved Cammie's idea for our wedding and we narrowed down a date too. 22nd July, it was a Friday and then a whole weekend of partying would be happening. She was adamant that she didn't want a honeymoon but I had a plan up my sleeve.

Prez slammed the gavel down. "First up, VP here is getting married in one month. Talk to Cammie and Ashlyn, make sure she has everything she needs. Second, Titch saved Cammie's ass a few weeks ago and by the sounds of it she was already pregnant too. VP wants him patched in, let's vote." Prez went around the table.

"Yay," Solar answered

"Yay," Toes agreed.

"Yay." Tat nodded. It went around the room and everyone voted to patch him in.

"Third, the guys from Cardiff Carvers were picked up by the police, they are all in lock up. Good work, Hitch."

"I'd like to propose something." He looked at Prez to see if it was ok and he nodded his head. "I'd like to vote on having my VP patch back."

"What the fuck!" I shouted.

"VP, calm down," Prez said. "Let's take a vote." Prez went around the table again and I had obviously done some good to this club as they all voted against Hitch being VP.

"Any other business?" Prez asked, he was met with silence. "Tat, get Titch in here." We waited in silence and I was furious that Hitch felt like he could claim his VP patch. I worked tirelessly for this club and protected everyone in it. Titch hobbled into the room behind Tat, he didn't need crutches anymore but he did walk with a slight limp.

"Congratulation, Titch," Prez said as he threw him a patched in leather cut. "You did some great work protecting the VPs Old Lady."

"Thanks, I'd do it all over again."

"This calls for a party. Enjoy boys." He slammed the gavel down and the room emptied.

I headed straight for the bar and ordered a whiskey, I could feel Cammie's eyes on me and within seconds her body was close to mine.

"You ok?" I pulled her close and placed my lips on her neck, the beat of her pulse calmed me and I needed that more than the whiskey.

"Yeah…" My phone began ringing and I pulled it out of my pocket to see it was my mum. "Mum, you ok?" I stepped away from the bar, leaving my whiskey sitting there. "What? Shit. I'm on my way." I looked around until I saw Tat and Solar. "Tat, Solar, let's ride." I kissed Cammie briefly and rushed out of the door and jumped onto my bike, waiting for Tat and Solar. I started up my Softail and the next thing I knew Cammie was climbing on the back, wrapping her arms around me.

"Cam, get off. I need to go." I tried pulling her hands apart but she wouldn't let go.

"I'm coming too."

"You're pregnant." I didn't want to risk hurting her but I needed to get to mums house, she said on the phone that Emily's dad had turned up and is demanding to see her. "Hold on fucking tight." I turned slightly and placed my helmet on her head, then we were heading down the road, faster than I would normally go with Cammie on the back but I couldn't risk anyone hurting mum or taking Emily away. We pulled up on the driveway and I noticed a car sitting on the side of the road. Cammie quickly climbed off and I held her hand as we ran up the steps and in through the front door.

"Oh, Mason. Thank God. These men are refusing to leave." I looked over towards mum's sofa and there were two men. One looked like he was in his early fifties, he was in a black suit and had short dark hair, blue eyes and a scar covering his right cheek. The other one was much younger, I'd say in his early thirties, he wore a dark blue suit, wasn't as clean shaven and had black hair and the start of a tattoo was peeping out of his shirt collar.

"What the fuck are you doing here?" I snarled, looking at the younger one.

"Don't look at me, I'm just the bodyguard." He said holding his hands up in surrender.

"Nanny?" Emily called from the top of the stairs. Cammie moved quickly, running up the stairs to stop Emily coming down. "Auntie Cammie, will you read me a story?"

"Of course I will."

"Talk," I growled looking at the older man. He stood up to face me and so did his bodyguard. Tat and Solar moved in closer behind me.

"I've come for my daughter. Simple as that." He crossed his arms over his chest.

"And you just expect us to hand her over? Simple as that?" I asked using his own words.

"She is mine!" he growled.

"We want proof. I don't for a second think my sister would have ever been with someone like you. What do you even do for a living? When and where did you meet her?"

"We met just over four years ago in London. I'm a business man, I have my fingers in a lot of pots. Katie was at this bar one night and we just hit it off from there." Shit, this couldn't be happening.

"What's your name? Why now? Why not four years ago?" He

reached into the pocket on the inside of his jacket and all three of us drew our guns out. Mum screamed and this guy laughed.

"I'm getting my business card." He passed it to me. Martin Clarke.

"Mum has full custody, you're not on the birth certificate. We will be fighting to keep that custody. You need to provide proof that she is yours. DNA test." I passed the business card to Tat and gave him a look, we were all really good at having conversations without even speaking. He knew what I needed, I needed information on this guy and quick. Tat stepped outside to call Toes.

Martin gave his bodyguard a look and he nodded his head.

"We'll be in contact when we have the relevant information that you need. But mark my words, I'll be taking my daughter with me, soon." Mum sobbed from across the room. I'd do anything in my power so it wouldn't come to that.

Solar walked them out and mum broke down in my arms, this was something that we always feared but we figured as no one had contacted us in four years that no one was interested in finding her.

"VP?" Tat called from the front door, I looked over mum's head at him and he nodded towards his phone.

"Hey." Cammie smiled as she walked down the stairs. "She's asleep." I moved from mum to Cammie and kissed her on the top of her head.

"I'll just be outside for a minute." She nodded and joined mum on the sofa, I heard mums cries again as I closed the front door. "What you got?"

"This guy is very dodgy, according to Toes and his connections. He has been known to dabble in prostitution, human trafficking, drug trade and child trafficking."

"Fuck!" I roared. "Let's hope like hell that he isn't her father.

If he is then we'll need a major plan. She will not be going to live with him, she will not be sold to the highest bidder."

"Mason." I looked over my shoulder to see Cammie standing in the doorway, shit, how long had she been standing there.

"We're talking here, privately," I snapped at her. She looked from me to Tat and Solar and knew that she couldn't answer me back.

"I was just telling you that your mum has gone to bed. I'll call Ash to pick me up." She turned away from me, digging her phone out of her jeans pocket.

"Cam, I won't be long. Just wait inside for me." She didn't turn around, didn't nod she just carried on in through the door, closing it behind her. "Bring this to church, get everyone you know on it. I'm staying here tonight."

"Got it," Solar said and Tat slapped me on the shoulder. I dug a cigarette out of my pocket and inhaled the nicotine as I watched them ride away. I just wanted a few calm months to marry my woman and wait for our baby to arrive, no such fucking luck. Mayhem as always.

I walked back through mum's front door and locked it behind me and turned off the outside light, I looked over to the sofa and Cammie was laying on it, fast asleep. I gathered her up in my arms and began walking up the stairs.

"Mason?" Mum said, coming out of the bathroom.

"We're going to crash here tonight," I said as I walked to the end of the hall where my bedroom was.

"Thank you. Goodnight. I love you."

"Love you too. Mum?" She turned around and looked at me. "It will all be ok, I promise." She nodded her head and pursed her lips. We both knew that we would have a fight on our hands in the future.

Chapter 29

Mason

Today was finally the day, the day that I got to make Cammie my wife. We were getting married in thirty minutes and I was fucking shitting it. We had the twenty week scan last week and everything was great, the doctor accidentally let slip that we were having a boy and Cammie cried her heart out. Later that night, she confessed to me that having another boy made her feel more worried and that she didn't want to forget Noah. I assured her that he would never be forgotten. She was still not so patiently waiting for him to start kicking her and she worried nearly every day that something was wrong.

We managed to find more information on Martin Clarke, incriminating evidence fell into our hands and we used it to our advantage. Blackmail wasn't normally a road we went down, but if that's what it took to save my niece from someone like him then so be it.

I was currently standing in the large garden area we had at the back of the clubhouse, the guys had mowed it all down, set up a small archway that Ashlyn covered in flowers and set up a few chairs for family members to sit on. The bikers were all going to park their bikes front tyre to back tyre until a circle was formed. Apparently, Cammie called it the 'Circle of Love' and we would be standing inside that circle with Prez, who was performing the ceremony. There would be an entrance to the circle, where Cammie had a sign made up saying 'Choose a seat not a side, we're all family once the knot is tied' and the bridesmaids would be brought in on bikes. We had a sound system in place for music and the bunnies would be serving drinks afterwards.

"Look at you, my handsome boy," Mum said as she walked over and placed her hands on my face. "Mason, you could have worn a tux and shaved." Mum shook her head in annoyance.

"Cammie wanted me to wear this and she doesn't like me clean shaven." I was wearing my smart dark blue jeans that apparently made my ass look great – her words, not mine. A black shirt with a couple of buttons opened and my cut. I had no idea what she would be wearing, she didn't let on about anything. If she would be in a traditional wedding dress, white, cream, red, black who the fuck knows. But one thing for sure, I bet she would look stunning.

The sound of engines had me looking around, one after another in came all my brothers, prospects and brothers from other chapters and clubs. Heather was Cammie's maid of honour, Ashlyn was a bridesmaid and Emily and Kelsey were flower girls.

Blade came in next on his Softail, slowly, with Tegan perched in front of him, he had one hand controlling the bike and one keeping her in place. She squealed with happiness, clapping her hands. Tat rode in behind him in the same position with Liam and he was chilled out and relaxed, a great addition to the club he will be when he is older. Just like I hoped my son would be.

The music started and Blade and Tat dropped Tegan and Liam off with my mum and went back towards the clubhouse. Blade came back with Heather perched on the bike sideways behind him, she was in a long, fitted ice blue dress, her hair was tied up with curls hanging down her face and bright red lips. Blade gave her a kiss as she hopped off and he drove back to the clubhouse, Tat headed over next with Ashlyn on the back of his bike, sitting the same way that Heather was and she wore exactly the same, her hair was done the same and she was also sporting the bright red lipstick. Next, Blade and Tat brought in Kelsey and Emily, they were sitting in front of them gripping hold of the handle bars and both of them were laughing. Once they were lifted off the bikes, they walked up the small aisle and sat in a seat. Blade and Tat circled around to fill the circle. It looked like everyone was here, if that was true, how was Cammie getting here? I looked around the formed circle again and no one was missing, my head shot up when I heard the roar of a bike and there she was my gorgeous Cammie riding in on a bike by herself, fuck me did she look hot doing that. I didn't even know she could ride. Once she was at the start of the aisle, she climbed off, straightened out her dress, kicked off her bikers' boots and proceeded to walk down the aisle to me in bare feet. The guys roared their bikes until she was standing in front of me and Prez made a cut off sign with his hands to quieten them down.

"Well, here we are…" Prez started. I looked into the bright blue eyes that was standing opposite me, she was breath taking in her pure white wedding dress, it was much shorter in the front coming above her knees and flowed out behind her until it hit the floor. The top part was fitted, no sleeves or straps and her breasts that seemed to be getting bigger every day were begging to be released; they teased me, showing off far too much cleavage. Her small baby bump was just noticeable through the dress.

"Mason…" Prez said my name and I looked at him, annoyed that he had interrupted my perusal of my future wife. "Your promises."

"Cammie…"

"Oh." She cut me off placing her hand on her tummy.

"What? What is it?" I asked panicked, looking at my mum for help when I noticed that Cammie had the biggest smile on her face.

"He kicked me." She laughed. "Here." She grabbed my hand and placed it on her tummy, I couldn't feel anything. "Go ahead, leave your hand there."

"Cammie... Oh, I felt it." I smiled and she laughed. "As soon as I saw you, I knew you were the one for me. Your blonde hair and bright blue eyes drew me to you but when I spent time with you, I fell and I fell hard. I promise to love you and our children for ever, I promise to always make you smile, I promise to protect you and most importantly I promise to cherish you. I'm happy to be spending my life with you." I reached over with my free hand and slipped the ring on her hand and wiped away her tears.

"Cammie, your promises," Prez said.

"Mason, I love you more than words can express, you're my whole entire life, and this one. I promise to love you and all of our children, I promise to take care of you, I promise to respect you and your brothers and most of all I promise to cherish you. I love you." She pushed the ring on my finger and I couldn't be happier.

"VP." Prez nodded at me to add my final bit.

"I promise to treat you as good as my leather, and ride you as much as my Harley." I winked at her and all the guys revved their engines. Cammie laughed, her head tipping back and Prez announced us husband and wife. I hooked my arm around her waist and pulled her close to me, placing my other hand on her face to tilt her head so I could take advantage of her lips. Heather and Ashlyn stayed with Cammie last night, claiming tradition that we couldn't see each other before the wedding. I missed having her next to me and I missed kissing her goodnight and good morning. Cammie decided that she didn't want her mum or dad at the wedding, she felt like as they had ignored her for a large part of her life that they didn't get to participate in her happy day. She struggled with the decision on whether to invite just her mum as she was there for her when she needed her the most, when Noah was born, but shortly after things went back to normal and she felt like a ghost living in their house and that was why she left. So she made the decision to keep them out of it.

We stayed around in the clubhouse for a little while, eating, drinking and dancing and every time I looked at Cammie she had this most amazing smile on her face, which caused my heart rate to pick up.

"You're pussy-whipped, man." Toes laughed as he stood beside me, sipping on his drink.

"When it's fine pussy like that I am no way going to complain." I chuckled. Cammie's head shot up from her drink and her eyes darted around the room looking for me, once her gaze settled on mine she placed her hand on her tummy and smiled. I think that was her way of telling me that our son was moving.

"Now, I'm going to steal her away for a couple of days. See you later, brother." I slapped him on the back and made a bee line for Cammie. She was sitting on the stool at the bar talking to Ashlyn and Heather. I walked up behind her and placed my hands on her hips, squeezing gently. "Wanna get out of here?" I whispered in her ear and her skin pebbled under my lips. She turned her head and smiled at me, nodding gently. I claimed her lips in a quick kiss and helped her off of her stool. Before we left, I turned towards the crowd of people that had made our day a special one.

"Listen up!" I shouted, waiting for everyone to give us their full attention. "I'm going to whisk my bride away but we just wanted to thank each and every one of you. Without you, this day wouldn't have been what it was. Stay, eat, drink and have fun. See you in a few days."

"Let's have a toast, once more to VP and Cammie!" Solar called out raising his glass in the air, everyone followed suit and it made my chest swell with pride that I could call all these people our family.

Chapter 30

Mason

I had whisked Cammie away for a three day break to St. Ives. It was peaceful and romantic, our view the whole time was the sea and she loved it. We spent hours making love, walking along the beach and eating out at restaurants, I was gutted when we had to come home early. Prez had called and told me we had a lead on finding Switch and I wanted to be very involved in that man hunt. Cammie didn't mind and she said she was keen to get home too as she missed her babies – the dogs.

We arrived back home about seven in the evening and I dropped Cammie off at home and headed straight for the clubhouse.

"It was a dead end, man," Toes told me as I took my seat to the left of Prez.

"You already went?" I asked, looking at him and then around to Prez.

"Yeah, we didn't want the trail to run cold but he always seems to be one step ahead of us. We can't seem to pin him down. Fucker," Prez explained, banging his fist down onto the table in frustration.

"What's the plan now?" Tat asked.

Everyone carried on talking and my mind drifted to Cammie and our wedding night.

"Mason, are we staying here?" Cammie asked in awe, staring up at the lavish hotel.

"Only the best for my wife." I leant towards her and kissed her on the side of her neck as she gazed at the tall, white hotel that sat in

front of us. It had a large front door, a couple of benches outside that looked out to the sea. A large garden sat at the side of the building, the grass was bright green and colourful flowers were dotted around.

"Say that again." She smiled.

"Wife," I whispered as I trailed my lips ever so gently across her skin at her neck.

"Mmmm, Mason?" I pulled back and looked at her. "Get me upstairs, now." The desire in her eyes was clear and I promised to always give my wife what she needed. I climbed out of the car and jogged around to her side of the car to help her out. We held hands as I pulled our one suitcase out of the boot and we walked up the few steps and pushed the front door open.

"Wow," Cammie gasped, we were met with a large marbled floor entrance with a sleek black desk to the right hand side and chrome lifts to the left. I tugged on Cammie's hand and led her to the reception desk.

"Hi, can I help you?" The young blonde woman smiled at me, showing off all of her white teeth.

"Yeah, we have a reservation for Mr and Mrs Cole." She smiled and tapped away on her computer, I didn't miss the way she was looking at me, undressing me with her eyes, I was sure it was the leather jacket that attracted so many people to me.

"Oh, yes, here it is. The honeymoon suite." She sounded disappointed. What did she think? She would smile her pearly whites at me and I was going to leave my wife standing there, in her wedding dress while I bent her over the desk and fucked her.

"The honeymoon suite?" Cammie gasped.

"Yes, sweetheart." I pulled her to my side as close as possible and kissed her lips. "After all, it is our honeymoon." I turned back to the receptionist. "We'd also like to not be disturbed."

"Of course, Mr. Cole." She placed our key card on the desk in front of me. "It's on the top floor, take the left hand lift, scan this card and it will open up into your room."

"Thank you."

"Enjoy your stay!" she called out after we started walking away. Once we arrived to our room, Cammie headed straight for the bedroom and called out my name. I pulled the suitcase along behind me, the bedroom was huge. It had patio doors that led out onto a balcony, matching white wardrobe and drawers and a massive bed that was covered in a white and red duvet set with rose petals covering it.

"Can you please unzip me?" Cammie asked as she pulled the pins out of her hair and it tumbled and bounced around her shoulders. I shrugged out of my cut and hung it over the red velvet chair that was in the corner of the room. I kicked my boots off one at a time as I walked towards her. The skin at the top of her back was too tempting not to kiss, she had caught a slight tan after working at the beach for the last six weeks, I had begged her to stop now that she was pregnant but, as stubborn as my woman was, I knew what the answer would be and she surprised me by saying that when she got to thirty weeks she would stop, that gave her one more month to work.

I slowly unzipped her dress, kissing down her back as I went, I was expecting to see some sexy underwear and was pleasantly surprised to see that all she had worn on our wedding day was a wedding dress.

"Fuck, Cam," I cursed as the zip stopped just above the curve of her ass. "Turn around." She slowly turned to face me, her hands were holding up the front of her dress so that it wouldn't fall down and I pulled up the bottom of her dress to see that she was in fact bare for me. I leant in and kissed the smooth skin of her pubic bone, holding onto her hips to keep her steady.

"Mason," she sighed as she parted her legs. I could see she was glistening and my resolve faded fast and my tongue was on her, pushing her lips apart so I could find her clit. I licked, sucked and nibbled all of her. When I felt her legs beginning to tremble I stopped and she complained.

"Lie on the bed." She went to pull her dress off and I stopped her. "Leave the dress on." She got comfy on the bed. Her legs dangled over the side and I knelt in front of her, spreading her legs wide. I smoothed my rough hands up the inside of her legs and watched as she became wetter. "You feeling ok?"

"No," she moaned, shaking her head.

"What's wrong?" I smiled, knowing full well the anticipation of me touching her was getting to her.

"Mason, please. Please stop teasing me," she begged, trying to hook her leg over my shoulder to pull me close to her. Her hips started gyrating in the air, she needed friction and I grabbed hold of her wrist as her fingers came to her clit.

"No touching," I scolded her.

"Then you do it, please." Her ass was wiggling on the bed and that made me smile, I loved knowing that just looking at her made her horny. I dipped my head and stroked my tongue over her opening, her legs quivered and with that one taste I was addicted, I threw her legs over my shoulder and she crossed her ankles behind my head. As I licked and sucked her, she used her legs to pull me closer and closer, rubbing her hot pussy all over my face.

"Mason... I..." she panted, I thrust two fingers into her and rubbed at her front wall, within seconds she was crying out my name and coming all over me. I used my free hand to unbuckle my jeans and push them down my hips. I was hard as fuck and needed to feel her, I loved the feeling of her pulsing around me, squeezing the head of my dick.

I pushed her legs apart once more, I looked up to see her arm thrown over her eyes and her chest moved rapidly. I stepped out of my jeans and removed my socks, kicking it all to the side of the bed. I yanked my shirt off over my head, I couldn't be bothered with undoing buttons. I pulled at her dress and it slipped off her body, revealing all her silky skin to me. I kissed down her neck, over her large breasts, suckling on her nipples which had her back arching off the bed and she removed her arm from her eyes so she could watch me. I ran my *hands over her baby bump that was growing every day. I got back onto my knees and pushed myself into her, inch by inch. She was warm, wet and still pulsing. I reached up for her hands and once she squeezed my hands I had her sitting up and I pulled her down onto my lap as I sat back on my heels. Our bodies were now touching, hot skin against hot skin. Her nipples were pebbled and the feel of them moving over my naked chest caused tingles in my spine. I wrapped my arms around her waist and her arms circled my shoulders. She kissed me as she rocked her body back and forth on my erection. Our tongues collided, our teeth clashed and I gripped hold of her hips, encouraging her to change her movements; I needed her to move up and down. Her movements were slow and I could feel every part of her, I sucked her bottom lip into my mouth and she moaned. Her rhythm got faster and she cried out every time my barbell piercing hit her clit. Our mouths were still touching, not kissing but gasping as the start of our orgasms started hitting us. I helped her move faster and faster, and once her legs started shaking, I pushed her so that the top of her back was leaning against the side of the bed for support and holding her slightly above me I started thrusting up into her, watching her breasts bounce. I felt her pussy tightening and she grabbed hold of her breasts and started tweaking her nipples.*

"That's it, baby. Come for me," I panted. My rhythm didn't stop and I chased her orgasm with my own. I released her hips and she pressed her body back against mine, rocking her body gently over mine pulling every last bit of my release from me.

"I love you," she whispered into my ear.

"I love you too, sweetheart."

I hid my now fully hard cock under the table and tried to concentrate on what was being said.

"I've contacted everyone I know, no one has heard anything from him," Toes explained. "Everyone seems to think the Satan MC no longer exist."

"Maybe it's time to contact charters from overseas. We will not rest until he is caught." Prez slammed down his gavel and

I was glad to be getting out of there. I needed to be home and with my wife. I quickly scrambled out of the room and headed straight for my bike, threw my leg over the seat and pushed my helmet on my head. Drake opened the gate enough so I could get through and I was eager to re-create our wedding night with Cammie.

I parked my Harley next to Cammie's car and looked up to the house to see that all the lights were off except for our bedroom one. She must have decided on an early night. I grabbed my keys and quickly unlocked the front door, stepping in and locking it behind me. I toed off my boots, leaving them at the bottom of the stairs. I didn't call out to her, I wouldn't wake her if she was already asleep. The bedroom door was ajar and pushed it open and stepped in, the sight before me had my blood turning cold. Cammie was sitting up in bed with a tight tank top on, that covered her bump, her hands were resting on it and tears were streaming down her face.

"Cam?" I said almost hesitantly. Her head shot up to look at me and she shook her head as her lip trembled. I rushed towards her and sat on the bed beside her. "Sweetheart, what's wrong?"

"It's happened again, I've done it again. I'm being punished."

"I don't understand."

"He's not moving, I can't feel him, Mason." She grabbed my hand and placed it on her tummy, I moved it around and couldn't feel him kicking either.

"Let's get you to the hospital." I tried to stay as calm as possible, knowing that if she lost this baby too that I would lose her. She would let the darkness claim her. I tugged the duvet off of her and grabbed her leggings that were beside the bed, helping her into them and pulled one of my hoodies over her head.

"I can't..." She pushed me away from her. "I can't do it... I can't hear those words again, Mason. I can't."

"It'll be ok." I pulled her against my chest and she cried. I rubbed my hand over her head and my chest constricted. I was scared. "Come on." I placed one hand on her back and the other under her knees and carried her down the stairs, only stopping to slip on my boots. She reached up and unlocked the door and I had her buckled into the car within minutes, running back up the steps to lock the house back up.

***

Cammie

I willed our son to move for the whole car journey. Mason was quiet and he kept one hand on my leg as he drove. We pulled into the hospital and I stared up at the grand building, not wanting to get out of the car. Mason pulled my door open and helped me out, I felt like I was in a daze, like I was a different person watching all of this unfold. That if I didn't believe this was happening then everything would be ok. Mason led me into the reception by the hand and I looked around at all the people that were sitting in the reception. Some were waiting to be seen, some had cuts on their hands, sick children on their laps and others were staring into space with tears running down their faces. I could hear the distant sound of Mason talking but I couldn't make out what he was saying.

"Cam?" I looked up at him and he wound his arm around my back and led me to a set of lifts. "We need to go to the third floor, they know we're coming." I stood beside him clutching hold of his hand, I felt like a zombie following obediently behind him. He'd done all the talking and I stood quietly beside him. It wasn't until I was laying on a hospital bed and the doctor in front of me kept asking questions did I realise that this was really happening to me.

"Cammie?" I looked up when Mason said my name. He nodded his head to the doctor and I looked at her. She was an older woman, with dark black hair and mesmerizing blue eyes.

"Cammie, when was the last time you felt him kick?" She was fiddling with the machine in front of her as she asked these questions.

"I... I don't remember."

"That's ok, let's have a look." She pushed my top off my tummy and squeezed some gel onto it, moving around the wand. I held my breath not wanting to hear her say those words when the most amazing sound filled the room. His heart was beating, I exhaled my held breath and burst into tears.

"He's ok?" I sobbed.

"Yes, he's doing very well." She angled the screen towards us so we could see.

"Why couldn't she feel him?"

"My guess would be that he was sleeping, but you are a little dehydrated you need to keep your fluids up. If you find yourself in this situation again try eating something sweet, drinking a cold drink and making lots of noise. If your baby doesn't respond to this then come back."

"Thanks, doc," Mason said gripping hold of my hand. "You ok, Cammie?" I looked up at him and nodded. "Let's get you home."

Chapter 31

Cammie

I was lying on the sofa after finishing my shift at work, concentrating on the baby. I wasn't sure if I had felt him move again and I didn't want to go back to the hospital just after being there last week. I was panicked.

"Hello?" Mason answered his phone.

"I can't feel him moving," I blurted.

"Sweetheart, have you tried eating something sugary or a really cold drink?"

"No, I forgot about that." I climbed to my feet and walked into the kitchen. Dusty jumped around my feet and I had to concentrate not to trip over her. I opened the back door and she flew outside. I rummaged through the cupboard until I found some chocolate and poured myself some water and grabbed some ice cubes from the freezer. I sat on the stool by the breakfast bar.

"Do you want me to come home?"

"No," I told him as I took a bite of the chocolate. "Where are you anyway?"

"It's a surprise." I could hear him mumbling to someone else, it sounded like he had covered the phone so I couldn't hear. "Any movement yet?"

"No." I took a sip of the ice cold drink. "Oh wait... Yes. Thank God." I sighed in relief. How was I going to cope like this for the next seventeen weeks?

"Great, I'll be home in two hours. I need you to be showered and ready for me, we're going out."

"Where are we going? What shall I wear?" I sat up straighter in my seat.

"It's a surprise and I'll bring something for you to wear."

"Ok." I smiled. "I can't wait."

"Love you," he said and ended the call.

I had two hours and we were going out, I think a nap was needed and then I'd start getting ready. I got the dogs in, gave them a treat each and headed upstairs for a lie down.

***

"Cam?" Mason called out as he walked in through the partially open bedroom door. He was looking sexy in a black tux, with a white shirt and black dickie bow tie.

"Wow, look at you?" I smiled. "What's the occasion? You didn't even wear a tux on our wedding day." I sauntered towards him and placed my hands on his chest. I was almost ready, my hair was straightened and kept down, just the way Mason liked it. I had put on neutral make-up as I didn't know what colour dress I was going to be wearing and my usual red lipstick that Mason also loved.

"I have a present for you." He passed me a box, hooking a dress bag up on the back of the bedroom door. I sat down and opened the box.

"What's this?"

"It's a baby foetal Doppler heart monitor. We can hear the baby's heartbeat with this. So if, for any reason, you're unsure if you felt him move or just want to be sure, you can use this." I was stunned, he knew the fears I battled with daily and although I had been to a few counselling session, I was still terrified that I was going to lose our baby.

"Oh, Mason. Thank you." I stood up and wrapped my arms around him. I tilted my head back, offering him my lips and he didn't disappoint. He pressed his lips gently to mine, making sure that he didn't ruin my make-up.

He grabbed the dress bag from the door and held it to me. "I need you to wear this, and we'll be leaving in ten minutes. I have shoes for you downstairs."

"Ok." I laid the bag on the bed and began to unzip it as Mason left the room. I gasped in surprise as I saw the material, it was silver and glittery. I held the dress up to me and looked at myself in the floor length mirror, it would show off my bump perfectly. I pulled the zip down at the back of the dress, untied my dressing gown and let it fall to the floor. I stepped into the dress and shimmied it up my body. The material was soft and silky and it had a built in bra, though I wasn't convinced it would hold me in since my breasts had grown so much in the last few weeks. I reached behind me and pulled the zip up. At the back, it ended just below my shoulder blades and it was strapless. It flowed to the floor and clung to my hips, tummy and bum. I turned around to catch a glimpse of the back, making sure my bum didn't look too big. Mason was always telling me that from behind I didn't even look pregnant. I was glad that it was the end of July and still fairly warm as I didn't have a jacket to go with a dress like this. I was excited to see where we were going. I grabbed my black clutch bag and headed out of the bedroom and down the stairs. Mason was standing at the bottom waiting for me, I picked the end of my dress up in my hand and Mason met me half way offering me his hand.

"You look amazing. Do you like the dress?"

"Yes, thank you."

"Do you want to wear flat shoes or heels?" He pointed to two pairs of silver shoes on the floor, one were ballet flats and the others were a four inch heel, sandal with a buckle with intricate diamante detailing.

"Definitely the heels." I smiled and he got down onto one knee and helped me put them on.

"Good choice." He smiled as he kissed the inside of my ankle. Beep. Beep. Beep.

"What's that?" I asked placing my foot back on the floor.

"That's our lift." He held his arm out to me and I placed my hand in the crook of his arm. He pulled the door opened and I squealed when I saw the long black limo sitting at the end of our driveway.

"Is that for us?" I asked as he gently pushed me outside, locking the door behind us.

"Yes." We proceeded towards the limo and before he opened the door, I reached up to his ear and whispered;

"I may just have to get on my knees in that limo and thank you in a good way." He shuddered underneath my touch. He pulled open the door and I was greeted by the sound of laughter, I looked inside and the limo was full of our friends. I glanced back at Mason and he winked at me. "Or not," I mumbled to myself. I climbed inside to find Heather and Blade dressed up like us, Blade was also in a tux and Heather was wearing a fire engine red long dress. Ashlyn was there too in a dark blue floor length dress with ruffles around the top and on the sleeves and Toes, Tat, Solar and Drake sat in smart trousers, shirts and their cuts. I laughed to myself how their jackets were almost like their security blankets. I was surprised to see that Mason and Blade weren't wearing theirs.

"Where are we going?" I asked, looking around at everyone as the limo started moving.

"Our lips are sealed," Heather said. "You look amazing, how's my nephew?" She asked, rubbing her hand on my tummy.

"He's good." Heather and I were so close, practically like sisters and she always referred to me as auntie Cammie to her kids. I was happy to be able to do the same when this little one was born.

Everyone, except for me, had a glass of champagne and I had sparkling water, the conversation was flowing around us and I was happy that everyone was together. I didn't get to see as much of Heather as I would like to. The car slowed down and I looked out the car window to see we had stopped in front of a large hotel. Everyone filed out and Mason held my hand as we walked towards the large set of doors. Once we were inside, there was a large sign displaying the event we were attending.

'SANDS (Stillbirth & neonatal death charity) charity auction'
I stopped walking and looked around at everyone, they all stopped and looked at me.

"Cam…" Heather began and Mason held up his hand to stop her.

"Go on in, we'll be just a minute." They all carried on in to the lavish ballroom, music was drifting out to us and I caught a glimpse of people dancing.

"I can't go in there." I backed away from Mason and he held my hand in a tight grip.

"Why can't you?" He bent his knees so he could look into my eyes.

"Look at me, I'm six months pregnant and you want to take me into a room where people have lost their babies. That's just not right."

"Cammie, you are one of those women. I thought this would be good for you, to talk to other people that have gone through what you have?"

"No, Mason. It won't feel right."

"I've been speaking to the lady in charge of this event, she knows what you went through and that we are expecting a baby boy and she is really keen to meet you." He pressed a kiss to my hand and I looked over his shoulder at the ballroom. People were laughing, joking and drinking. "It's just a room full of rich men and women who are raising money for a great cause."

"Ok, I'll try. But if I feel uncomfortable, we can leave?"

"Absolutely and we can get back to the promise of you giving me head in the limo." He laughed. I smacked him on the chest and he held hold of my hand and led me into the ballroom.

***

Mason

I was so very proud of Cammie, I knew she was worried about making other people feel uncomfortable but everyone was so kind to her. She had started talking to one woman, Pamela who gave birth to a still born and she herself was also pregnant. They moved off together to talk somewhere quieter a little while ago and I was now trying to find her.

I came across her talking to Cynthia, the organiser of this particular event. She was a lady in her early sixties, she had grey hair tied up into some sort of twist, a long flowing green ball gown and a silver clutch thing, one like Cammie had, that held their lipstick and shit in.

I sidled up beside Cammie and slipped my arm around her waist, kissing her on the side of her head. She smiled up to me and I took the hand Cynthia offered and kissed it politely. I didn't want to interrupt their conversation.

"I'd love to help out more," Cammie added. "How can I help?"

"Well, tonight is about building money for a new centre, one where mums and dads can feel comfortable coming and talking. We're looking to venture into the southwest."

"Wow, that's great." Cammie looked like she was thinking.

"This is an auction right?"

"Yes. We have several items donated from people and they can go around the room." She pointed to a set of tables. "And bid on the item you want. People have been very generous. There is a trip for two to Italy…"

"I want to donate…"

"That's very kind of you, but…"

"My boys." She nodded her head as the guys and Heather and Ashlyn started walking towards us. "Auction them off, for a date night."

"Whoa, hold on a minute," Toes complained.

"That's very generous and probably would go down well, they're all very handsome." Cynthia smiled.

"It's for a good cause, brother." I chuckled.

"You too," Cammie said to me and my face fell. Blade started laughing and Heather dug him in the ribs with her elbow.

"Oh look at that, Blade just volunteered himself." Heather smiled.

"What?" He looked at her, annoyance covering his face.

"This is a marvellous idea, Cammie. Thank you." Cynthia hugged her and then looked at all of us. "Follow me, boys."

"You better win," I growled at her.

"I don't have any money," she said gesturing with her hands.

"I'll sort it. Bid big, baby." I winked at her and followed the guy backstage.

Chapter 32

Cammie

"Hello, ladies and gentlemen," Cynthia began as she stood on the stage. "With thanks to Mrs. Cammie Cole, we have another auction about to take place. Ladies, gather around. This is for a date night with a badass biker." The crowd cheered and clapped and I loved how much the other women were up for this.

"Are you going to bid on Blade?" I asked Heather.

"Maybe, I haven't decided yet." She laughed, taking a sip from her cocktail glass. "What about you Ash? Gonna bid on one?" Heather asked.

"Maybe, just as it's a good cause."

"Here we go, ladies, first up is Toes, he's thirty two, a member of the Cornish Crusaders MC and he got his name from a fetish for women's feet. Turn around so they can see all the goods." She laughed and Toes did as she had asked. "Let's start the bidding at fifty pounds."

"Fifty quid?" he complained.

"One hundred pounds!" someone called out.

"A hundred and fifty!" A counter offer came in and it went on like that until he was sold for three hundred pounds.

"Wow, the ladies are loving this. Good idea, Cam," Heather praised me.

"Next up, ladies, is Holes. Now I have to tell you this one is a married man, he's also the Vice President of his biker club and his nickname comes from him being a piercer. Isn't he looking dashing in his tux?"

"Two hundred pounds!" someone called out and my head

whipped around to see who it was, did she not just hear Cynthia say he was a married man.

"Three hundred, take the jacket off!" someone else shouted.

"You heard them, jacket off." Cynthia smiled. Mason obliged and unbuttoned his jacket and let it fall down his arms.

"Four hundred. What does he have pierced?" I looked again and it was the same woman who bid first. Mason pointed to his eyebrow, lip and stuck his tongue out.

"Holy shit! Six hundred!" a woman called out who was obviously turned on by his piercings.

"You better save him," Heather told me.

"Seven hundred!" the first woman shouted.

"Fuck," I swore under my breath. "One thousand pounds."

"Sold!" Mason shouted, pointing at me and I laughed. It would definitely be money well spent.

The auction continued as Mason prowled over to me. "I hope you wasn't going to let someone else win me?" His hands were on my hips and my tummy was flat against him.

"Well, technically, you won yourself as I have no money."

"I'll lend it to you." He rose his eyebrows to his hairline whilst chuckling.

"That's Tat, Drake and Solar done!" Heather shouted to me, invading our bubble.

"Oh, how much did they make?"

"Tat went for five hundred. Solar for nine hundred and Ashlyn won Drake for four hundred."

"You bid on Drake?" Mason asked her.

"It's for a good cause, I'm only making sure I'm helping. I didn't want to get punched if I won Blade." She laughed.

"Ok, ladies, the last one of the evening. This is Blade, he is the President of the Devon Destroyers MC. He's also married with three kids."

"Hundred pounds."

"Two hundred."

"Three hundred."

"Five hundred."

"Seven hundred!" Heather called out.

"Eight hundred." We looked to the side and there was a tall slim woman with long dark straight hair in a black dress biding against Heather.

"Nine hundred." Heather bid.

"Twelve hundred." Every time she bid she looked at Heather with a smirk on her lips.

"Fifteen hundred!" Heather shouted.

"Sixteen hundred."

"Go big," I whispered to Heather.

"Two thousand five hundred!" Heather called out raising her hand in the air. Everyone's attention was on the other woman and she made a cut off sign with her hand and Cynthia declared Blade as sold.

"Thank you, ladies, what a great way to make some money. That's a further five thousand and six hundred pounds towards the charity." She started clapping and everyone joined in. I felt good, that was my good deed done for the day.

"You ok?" Mason asked as I leant into him.

"Tired." I yawned.

"Shall we go home?" I nodded and said goodbye to Heather and Ashlyn. They were going to stay for a bit longer.

"The limo will be outside for you," Mason told Blade and they did one of those manly handshake back slap things. We walked silently to the limo and before we got in, Mason turned to me.

"You need to re-do your lips. It's worn off a bit." He rubbed his thumb over the bottom of my lips and once we were sitting in the limo, I pulled out my small compact mirror and lipstick and re applied it. Mason pressed a button on the side of the door and the privacy screen started to raise between us and the driver. I looked at him and smiled.

"How tired are you?" he asked.

"Why?"

"How about getting on your knees and claiming the prize you won?" I placed my clutch bag on the side of the seat and dropped to my knees. Mason leant back against the chair and placed his hands on his thighs. I started to undo his belt and trousers.

"So if someone else won, is this what they would be doing to you right now?"

"Fuck no." I kissed the top of his cock and he groaned, I left my lipstick mark on him and I knew he loved seeing that. I closed my lips together and he nudged them apart with his cock. "Be a good girl and open up for me," he groaned. I stuck out my tongue and licked him from root to tip. I did this several times until his hand finally grasped onto my head; I loved him controlling the speed of my head. I opened up my mouth and he thrust inside, causing me to gag. He quickly pulled away and I sucked him back in again, making sure to swallow when I felt his head at the back of my throat.

"Fuck!" he swore. I looked up at him and his head was thrown back onto the seat headrest and his other fist was clenched tightly still resting on his thigh. I rose to my knees and sucked him in again, grabbing hold of his clenched fist, he loosened it, looking down at me and I placed it on my left breast and encouraged him to knead. He pinched my nipple and I moaned, the next thing I knew I could feel the warm air on my nipples, he had pulled the top of my dress down, exposing me to him.

"I love these breasts." He moaned as my speed increased.

"Fuck! Stop. On your feet." I pulled away from him and he helped me climb to my feet, I had to bend over slightly as we were in a moving car. His hands disappeared up my dress until he found my underwear and began pulling it down my legs, I stepped out of them and he threw them onto the seat beside him.

"Turn around," he said motioning with his finger at the same time. "Hands on the seat in front of you." I did as he told me to and then he was encouraging me to sit back onto him. "This is going to be fast. If it's too much, just tell me to stop." I nodded as he started pushing into me. Goosebumps covered my body as he grabbed my breasts in his hands and I sat upright onto him. I pressed one hand against the window as he lowered his legs and my feet flattened on the floor.

"Hold still," he told me and I was practically in a squat position over the top of him. He released my breasts and held onto my hips, his body moved under me, slamming up into me in a relentless rhythm. My hand was still pressed against the window and my other hand went to my bump. He was thrusting into me so fast and hard, I was on the verge of exploding before he had even got started.

"Mason, Mason, I'm going to come."

"Yes, come for me. Now." I let go and the warmth spread up through my body, my heart rate increased, my breathing shallowed and I was calling out his name. He was still pumping into me and then his release caused another orgasm to hit me and my legs shook, I couldn't hold myself up much longer. Mason quickly pulled out of me and settled me on his lap, my back to his chest. We didn't talk, our breathing was laboured and we both tried to control our trembling bodies.

Chapter 33

Mason

"Sweetheart, I've gotta head to the clubhouse!" I called out as I wandered down the stairs, I slipped on my biker boots and headed into the kitchen.

"What?" she asked as she had Dusty standing on the kitchen table and was brushing her coat.

"I've gotta head to the clubhouse. Church."

"Babe, we're supposed to be getting your son's room ready today. He'll be here in eight weeks. You need to build his cot and we still haven't settled on a name for him."

"That's because you don't like any of the names I choose."

"We are not calling him Mason junior." Dusty jumped off the table and Cammie crossed her arms over her chest, pushing her breasts up.

"We can shorten it to MJ."

"No way, people will think we named him after Michael Jackson." I stepped closer to her and wrapped my arms around her.

"We'll talk about it tonight. I've really gotta go. Call me if you need me." I kissed her quickly on the lips before I was rushing out of the door

***

"Everyone here?" Prez asked, looking around the room, then he slammed the gavel down. "Drake found this tied to the front gate this morning." Prez placed a piece of paper on the table and I looked up to see Drake was clenching his jaw and his hands curled in and out of fists. What was his problem?

"What is it?" Solar asked.

"It's definitive proof that he is still hanging around," Drake growled.

"Who?" I asked.

"Switch," Prez said sighing and shaking his head.

"What the fuck?" I grabbed the piece of paper and looked at it.

'You can't keep her from me. She'll always be mine. Those marks on her body proves that. Hand over Ashlyn and I won't bother you again.'

"Shit!" I roared. "How do we know this is definitely from him?"

"We just have to trust that it is," Prez said rubbing his hand over the back of his neck.

"What are we going to do?" Drake asked.

"There's only one thing." Prez slumped back into his seat and his eyes drifted over the table to each and every member, finishing on me. "We're a club, we protect what's ours. Ashlyn ain't an Old Lady, she ain't a club whore, but she came here for protection and she feels safe here with us. She's family. We protect her." There was murmurs around the table, everyone agreeing with him.

"This is what I propose, Drake takes her away from here, on his bike, someplace safe, until we can track him down. We'll form alliances with the other clubs, we will get this sick bastard. Drake, you do a great job and you'll be patched in. Let's take a vote."

"Yay." From Tat.

"Yay." From Solar, Toes, Titch.

"Yay." From Drake and myself.

"Nay." From Hitch. "He's only a prospect, he can't protect her."

"I can protect her and will."

"Seven over one. Drake goes."

"What do we tell her?" I ask.

"She has to know the truth," Drake adds. "It'll be safer if she knows."

"Agreed," Prez said as he slams down the gavel. I felt awful, I was pleased to know that he didn't want Cammie, but I didn't want him having Ashlyn either.

***

Cammie

Can you come to the clubhouse it's important x

That was the text I received from Mason a couple of minutes ago.

Yeah, on the way x

Jono, the new prospect, opened the gate for me as I pulled in, he had only been with the club for a month. He was only eighteen with a shaved head and tattoos covering it instead. He was smaller built than the rest of them but he gave off this don't mess with him vibe. As I climbed out of the car, Mason started walking towards me. I smiled at him and his jaw was tense.

"You ok?" I reached up to touch him and he buried his face into my neck, pressing his lips against my pulse and placing a hand onto our son.

"We need to talk," he mumbled.

"Ok." I hated it when anyone said that. He took my hand and led me to the swings in the park where Ashlyn and I had many talks before. I sat on the swing and Mason crouched down in front of me.

"Normally we wouldn't be telling you this but it's very important." I nodded at him to keep going. "We've heard from Switch." I gasped and covered my mouth with my hand.

"He wants Ashlyn, says that she's his."

"No," I whimpered.

"He will not get her. Drake is taking her away, on the bike, keeping her safe until we find him. Prez has called a lockdown, we don't want Switch thinking he can take anyone else and use them as a bargaining chip."

"What about the baby? What if I go into labour while we are on lockdown?"

"Then we'll get you to the hospital. No one is going to mess with my son being born."

"What about the dogs? Can we bring them with us?"

"No. Sorry, sweetheart. We'll drop them off at mums. Emily will love having them there."

"Ok," I softly said as my eyes filled with tears.

"Hey, please don't cry." He cradled my face in his hands and used his thumbs to brush away my tears.

"Yo, VP." I looked up and Drake was waving his arm and Ashlyn was standing next to his bike.

"Looks like they are ready to leave. Come on." He pulled me up from the swing and kissed me on the top of my head. "It'll all be ok." We walked over to where everyone was standing and I hugged Ashlyn tightly.

"Promise you'll be safe?"

"Drake will protect me," she assured me.

"You." I pointed at Drake. "Look after her."

"Don't worry, I will." He climbed on the bike and Ashlyn climbed on behind him.

"Keep an eye out, the slightest feeling that you're being followed, call us," Prez told him.

"Sure thing." They both placed their helmets on their heads and was soon zooming out of the compound.

Epilogue

Three years later

Mason

"Cam?" I called out as we walked into the house.

"Mummy?" Harley called out.

"Upstairs!" She called back and I picked up our soon to be three year old and ran up the stairs. I threw him onto the bed beside Cammie and he bounced around, giggling.

"You ok?" I asked, worriedly. Watching as Cammie used the baby heart monitor on her tummy.

"Yeah, he's ok. I just had a panic then for a minute. I'm sorry," she said as she wiped the gel off her tummy.

"You don't need to be sorry." I placed my hand on her face and gently kissed her lips, we would be a family of four in only a matter of months.

"Mummy, why you sad?" Harley asked as he climbed to his feet on the bed and pressed his hand onto her face much like I did.

"I'm ok, baby. Just checking to make sure your brother was ok."

"Oh." He tilted his head to the side and bent down and pressed a kiss on her tummy. "There, all better now."

"He sure is. Do I get one of those?" she asked pointing to her lips and he kissed her too.

"I need to pee," he called out as he went running towards our en-suite.

"You sure you're ok?" I asked her again, climbing up onto the bed beside her and pulling her into my side.

"Yeah, I just hate having that scared feeling. I'd keep that thing permanently attached to me if I could." She laughed. She still held the same fears of having another still born baby, she was terrified in the hospital the moment Harley was born, he was so chilled out that he didn't cry straight away and that put Cammie into a panic, tears were streaming down her face until they placed him in her arms and then she cried for a whole different reason. He was perfect with his red crinkly face, button nose and dark hair just like mine.

"Hello?" Mum called out.

"Nanny's here!" Harley called out running from the bathroom and out the bedroom doors.

"Careful on the stairs!" Cammie called out as she got to her feet and waddled away from me.

"You're so sexy. What did I do to deserve you?" I said as I crossed my ankles and laid back on the bed with my arms over my head.

"If you think this is sexy, you need your eyes checking." She laughed walking out of the bedroom door.

"Nothing wrong with my eyes."

I shot to my feet and caught up with her on the stairs, I kissed and nibbled her neck as we walked into the kitchen where mum was making a cup of tea.

"Hi, you two." Mum smiled. "Want a drink?"

"Yes please." Cammie smiled as she walked into the kitchen and gave mum a hug. Mum placed her hand on Cammie's tummy and rubbed it.

"That's a strong kick." She laughed.

"He knows his nanny." Cammie smiled again and I stood back and watched them all. Emily and Harley were sitting at the kitchen table colouring in, Dyson and Dusty were sleeping in their bed and Mum and Cammie were talking and laughing. This was what I always wanted, my own family.

The End

About the Author

Kacey Hamford is a pen name for me (Kelly). I am in my thirties and started this journey in 2014, I love to read romance books about rockstars, so thought I would have a go at writing one myself. I really enjoyed it and got a boost of confidence once my books started selling.

I have gone on to write a young adult series, set in a college. The series is still on going.

I also have this MC series, it was something different for me to write and I enjoyed it so much, especially when I got readers telling me they would love to read books about the sub characters.

I work full time as a dog groomer, I love to read and my friends and family are very important to me. They are all so supportive of my writing career and encourage me to carry on.

It still makes me happy to see reviews and sales going up. I love writing and hope to do it as more of a full time job in the future.

I would like to thank my friends for supporting me throughout the writing of this book. And finally a MASSIVE thank you to you, the reader for bothering to buy and read the book and making it all the way to the end to be reading this. Reviews are very important to authors so please leave a review where you bought it.

For information on upcoming books please go to:

https://www.facebook.com/pages/Author-Kacey-Hamford/572126959568554

Other book wrote by Kacey Hamford -

The Rocking Series:

Book 1. Rocking Esme

hyperurl.co/6p848k

Book 2. Rocking Scarlett

hyperurl.co/tjvgpx

Book 3 Rocking Marcy

hyperurl.co/ffymuj

Book 4 Rocking Ashton

hyperurl.co/9hrs7s

Book 5 Rocking Danni

hyperurl.co/tcitkv

Book 6 Rocking Noelle

www.amzn.co.uk/dp/B0184HLUGS

Chance Series

Book 1 - Taking A Chance

Hyperurl.co/puqylu

Book 2 – Giving A Chance

hyperurl.co/h6tezv

South Coast Brothers

Book 1 – Devon Destroyers MC

mybook.to/DevonDestroyers

Book 2 – Cornish Crusaders MC

mybook.to/CornishCrusaders